THE MYSTERY OF
THE MISSING FORMULA
A Star Original

... Klaus feinted with a left at Barton. The special agent moved away as the man then went for Snowey. Taken aback, the ex-sergeant was unable to do much. He fell to the ground as a blow landed in his stomach. Before he could recover, his attacker was racing away down the street.

'I should have hit him with my handbag,' Snowey said as he watched the retreating figure.

'It's no laughing matter,' Dick Barton announced.

'No sir,' Snowey replied.

'You're going to have to do better than that if we're to stay in business ...'

D1630899

Further books in the DICK BARTON series

DICK BARTON – SPECIAL AGENT

No. 2
THE MYSTERY OF
THE MISSING FORMULA

Mike Dorrell

A STAR BOOK

published by
the Paperback Division of
W. H. ALLEN & Co. Ltd

A Star Book
Published in 1978
by the Paperback Division of
W. H. Allen & Co. Ltd
A Howard and Wyndham Company
44 Hill Street, London W1X 8LB

Cover photo shows Tony Vogel and James Cosmo in a scene from
DICK BARTON – SPECIAL AGENT, A Southern Television
Production, in association with Demob Ltd

Printed in Great Britain by
Hunt Barnard Printing Ltd,
Aylesbury, Bucks

ISBN 0 352 30308 5

Chapter One

*After solving 'The Great Tobacco Mystery', Dick Barton,
Snowey White and Jock Anderson had a celebration in a
Mayfair nightspot. When Jock Anderson got out of Barton's
car after being given a lift home, a mysterious young girl
approached him. She was knocked down by an unknown
assailant who afterwards got away. Clutched in her hand
was half a British Army of Occupation banknote – a signal
to Jock Anderson that his former officer, George Cameron,
was in trouble. Dick Barton and Snowey took the girl back
to Barton's flat.*
   Now read on.

The girl woke up in a strange bed in a strange room. She
was about seventeen, she was pretty, and, if there had been
someone in the room with her they might have noticed that
she looked both innocent and slightly groggy. The innocence
was natural, but the grogginess had been induced by a figure
in a trilby and a leather trenchcoat who had knocked her
down in a dark street the night before.

Her name was Lucy Cameron. She was dressed only in her
underclothes and she didn't know where she was. She got
out of bed and walked around the room looking for her
clothes. They weren't in sight. All she could find on a chair
beside the bed was a dressing gown. It belonged to Dick
Barton.

Lucy put on the dressing gown and walked across the
room to where an ornate nineteen-thirties style mirror was
hanging on the wall. She examined herself in it. She had
an incipient black eye and a very professional-looking piece
of sticking plaster across her forehead. She didn't know how
it had got there. All she remembered was seeing Jock Ander-

son in the street the night before and running towards him clutching her father's half of a British Army of Occupation banknote. The rest was a blank.

She thought for a minute as she heard voices from the room beyond the door, then she tiptoed towards it and listened. After a few moments, she opened it cautiously and walked in.

Dick Barton looked up as the girl entered. He had been reading *The Express*. He saw that she was peering suspiciously at him. He tried to alleviate any feelings of alarm that she might have had. 'Hello young lady. How're you feeling?'

Lucy turned towards the man who had spoken to her. The other one in the room was bending over an ironing board on which he was pressing her clothes. 'Who are you?' she asked.

'My name's Dick Barton, and this is George White,' the special agent replied as he pointed towards his ex-sergeant. 'Commonly known as Snowey.'

Snowey looked up from his work. 'Wotcher,' he said. Then he noticed that the bruise around the girl's eye was worse than he had previously thought. 'My word, but you ain't half going to have a shiner,' he added.

Dick Barton put his newspaper down on the table in front of him. He turned towards the girl again. 'Well, are you going to tell us what all this is about?'

'What're you doing with my clothes?' Lucy was still looking towards the man in front of the ironing board.

Snowey White shrugged. 'I'm ironing them, aren't I? And I'd sooner the word didn't get around.' He picked the clothes up off the ironing board and held them out towards the girl. 'Here.'

She still didn't know who they were. Or how she had got into the flat. She was nervous. 'You so much as lay a finger on me and I'll scream the place down,' she warned Snowey.

The ex-sergeant was still holding out the bundle of clothes. 'There's gratitude for you,' he said.

Lucy Cameron snatched up her clothes and retreated to the bedroom. Once inside, she locked the door.

Dick Barton looked across at Snowey and winked. 'We're only trying to help,' he shouted.

There was a muffled reply from the other side of the bedroom door. 'I'm not coming out of here until you get Mr Anderson.'

Meanwhile, Jock Anderson himself, former Rolls-Royce mechanic, ex-private and current member of the Dick Barton team, was leaving his terraced house in a street in East London and heading for the nearest bus stop. He was heading for Dick Barton's flat in Chelsea. He was thinking about the sudden appearance of the other half of the British Army of Occupation banknote and the fact that his former officer, George Cameron, was in trouble. He didn't know that he was being tailed by the same figure in trenchcoat and trilby who had knocked Lucy down the night before. As yet, he didn't even know the girl's identity.

Lucy was sitting on the bed in Dick Barton's bedroom. She seemed to have been there for ages. But she had no intention of moving until someone she trusted arrived. She had wedged a chair under the door handle. She was still waiting. There was a knock at the door.

'Who's that?'

'It's Jock Anderson,' said the voice from the living room.

'Prove it.'

'Here's George Cameron's half of the Occupation note you were carrying.'

Lucy watched as the piece of paper that she had been carrying the night before slid under the door.

'Now here's mine.'

When the other half followed the first, Lucy picked them both up and joined them together. They fitted perfectly. She was almost convinced. She took the key out of the lock of the bedroom door. 'Stand back so's I can see you,' she ordered.

At the other side of the door, Jock Anderson looked towards Dick Barton and Snowey for guidance. The special agent shrugged.

'We've got a right one here, I can tell you,' Snowey commented.

7

Then Jock obediently stood back a few paces. Through the keyhole, he saw a beady eye staring at him.

After a while, Lucy spoke from the bedroom side of the door. 'All right. I'm coming out now.'

Jock, Snowey and Dick Barton heard the sound of the chair being taken away from the door and the key being turned in the lock.

'The relief,' Dick Barton said. He was amused.

'Decent of you,' Snowey chimed in.

Then the door opened, and Lucy appeared. She took a step into the room.

'Captain Barton and Snowey here are friends of mine,' Jock said as he waved towards his two friends.

'Well, I wasn't to know that, was I?' Lucy countered.

Dick Barton smiled at the girl. She was looking better than the last time he had seen her. 'Fair enough,' he admitted. 'You must be jumpy after last night.' He paused, reluctant to go into all the details. 'By the way, the doctor says there are no bones broken.'

While Barton spoke, Jock Anderson had been looking closely at the girl. But he still didn't recognise her, while feeling that there was something vaguely familiar about her face. 'How do you know me?' he said after a while.

Lucy's reply was prompt: 'From your photo, of course.'

'Which photo?'

'The one you had taken with Dad in Hamburg, silly.' She was laughing at Jock now.

'Dad?'

Lucy Cameron shook her head. 'Anybody'd think it was you had been bashed last night and not me. I'm George Cameron's daughter, Lucy, aren't I?'

'Well!' Jock said in amazement.

'You and him being such pals,' Lucy smiled again. 'Don't tell me you didn't know he had a daughter?'

Jock Anderson turned away, flushing slightly with embarrassment. 'Well of course. He was full of you. But from the way he spoke . . . ' he paused again. 'I pictured just a bairn.'

Lucy nodded. This time there was a more serious expression on her face. 'That's what this is all about, in a way.'

The special agent looked towards Snowey White. He

8

didn't want to intrude. 'Shall we take a walk, Snowey?' he suggested.

'What? Oh.' Snowey noticed that the governor was looking closely at him. 'Yes. Right.' He shifted his feet.

'Not on my account,' Lucy Cameron said firmly. 'Not if you and Mr Anderson are friends.'

'A team, more or less,' Jock stated.

'That was the idea, anyway,' Dick Barton put in.

'Well then,' Lucy said slowly. She smiled again. 'I wouldn't mind a cup of tea.'

'I'll see what I can rustle up.' Snowey began to make his way towards the kitchen.

Lucy now felt more relaxed. At least she was amongst friends.

But outside, in the street, the man with the trenchcoat and trilby, whose name was Klaus, and whose occupation was sinister, was finishing making a report into the telephone. He hung up, came out of the call box, and took up his station once again. He was keeping a close watch on Dick Barton's Somerset Mansions flat.

Lucy was now sitting at the table in Dick Barton's living room. She was finishing off a plate of bacon and eggs cooked for her by Snowey. Dick Barton was sitting across the table.

'That crack on the head doesn't seem to have done your appetite any harm,' the special agent remarked.

Lucy finished a mouthful. 'Here, I've eaten you out of house and home.'

'So long as you've enjoyed it,' Jock said from across the room.

'Oh, but I have.'

Snowey came in from the kitchen. 'That's the main thing,' he remarked.

Now that she had finished eating, Lucy Cameron took up her story once more.

'Anyway . . . we rented this place . . . and . . . well, going on seven years. I'd been a kid when Dad went away. This . . . it was like we'd both found a friend.' She paused for a moment. 'I'd got my Higher Cert., and time to kill before going up to University, so . . . sometimes I'd spend all day planning the evening meal. And then we'd talk – I mean, really talk.' She turned towards Jock Anderson. 'About you, where we'd been since Mum died, who we were, what we wanted to be. Playing house, I suppose,' her voice was full of regret. 'But it wasn't half lovely. Then . . . well one day . . . He just didn't come back from work.'

While Lucy had been speaking, Snowey White had wandered over to the window. Now he spoke to Dick Barton: 'Sir, there's a geezer out there clocking the place.'

Dick Barton crossed to the window and looked out. In the street, near the telephone kiosk, he saw a man in a leather trenchcoat and trilby trying to look as if he was a casual lounger.

'I spotted him right after Jock arrived,' Snowey added.

The special agent turned away from the window, and went across to where Jock and Lucy were sitting. He looked closely at the Scots mechanic. 'Were you followed?'

'Not as far as I know,' Jock replied, 'I wasn't looking for it, mind you. Why should I be?'

Dick Barton's face creased thoughtfully. 'The same reason as Lucy got set upon, perhaps. I don't know.' He looked across to Lucy. 'What did you do when your father didn't come back?'

Her reply was to the point. 'Phoned Mr Tibbs, that's his colleague at work, next day. He said he'd had to go off on a business trip.'

'Sounds plausible,' John Anderson commented.

'Perhaps,' Lucy added, but her voice sounded more doubtful. 'But the next time I phoned, Mr Tibbs said he'd left – gone off altogether. A business trip, perhaps.' She paused while she re-considered Tibbs's explanation. 'But he'd never have left, not without telling me.'

'You can't be sure of that,' Dick Barton said gently.

'I know him. I can,' Lucy insisted. Then she went across and picked up an envelope that she had left lying on the table. 'Besides, I got this the very next day.' She handed Barton the envelope.

The special agent took out the letter that was inside and began to read it out aloud: ' "Just to say don't worry. I'll explain everything soon. Enclosed to tide you over. Love." '

When he had finished, he looked in Lucy's direction once more. 'Money?' he asked.

The girl nodded in confirmation. 'And, in amongst it,' she said, 'was his half of that note.' She looked towards Jock. 'He's told me about your pact you see. He said, if we ever got in trouble not to contact the police or anybody else. Just you. You'd know what to do. When I got to your place you were out. I spotted this bloke hanging about. I thought I'd shaken him off and – well, you know the rest.'

Dick Barton pointed towards the other end of the room. 'Is that him?' Then, as Lucy walked towards it, he said, 'Don't get too close to that window.'

Carefully, Lucy Cameron peered out into the street. She recognised the man who looked up towards the flat and then away again. 'That's him all right,' she confirmed, turning back into the room.

Dick Barton was not alarmed by this piece of additional information. It was as much as he'd already expected. He rubbed his chin thoughtfully. 'So . . . either someone knew your father'd got a message to you, or expected that he would and . . . What's his job?' he finished.

'He went back to being a chemist, didn't he?' Jock Anderson said.

Lucy nodded in reply. 'With Mertons – the Southampton fertilizer firm.'

Barton was thinking fast. 'What exactly does he do there?'

'I don't know – exactly,' Lucy replied. 'But, I mean it's not like he was working on the atom bomb.'

'He could still be trying to contact you.' The special agent was convinced that it was more than a possibility. 'Let's get you home and Jock can stay with you while we try and find out just what's going on.'

'Yes, but how?' Jock could see Dick Barton's point. But he needed a more definite set of procedures.

'I should think the first thing is to give the firm a once over, and have a word with that colleague of his,' the special agent announced. He turned to Lucy, 'What's his name?'

'Albert Tibbs.'

Snowey was standing at the window once more. 'I hate to chuck a spanner in the works,' he said, 'but what do we do about Muggins?'

A few minutes later, Dick Barton came out of Somerset Mansions and looked around cautiously. He saw the figure in the trenchcoat across the road, but pretended that he didn't. Then, he turned towards the entrance of the flats and beckoned. A figure in a headscarf, slacks, and raincoat, came hurrying out. Dick Barton shielded the figure with his arm and they both hurried away.

Klaus, the man in the trenchcoat and trilby, began to tail them.

Dick Barton stopped around the nearest corner and waited. It didn't take long. Klaus raced around the corner and came to an agonised halt. He nearly bumped into the figure with the headscarf. But she, in spite of the clothes she was wearing, looked anything but feminine.

'You want to get your eyes tested, mate,' Snowey White said.

And then, from behind Snowey, Dick Barton confronted the other man. 'Now suppose you tell us just where you fit into all this,' he demanded.

Klaus feinted with a left at Barton. The special agent moved away as the man then went for Snowey. Taken aback, the ex-sergeant was unable to do much. He fell to the ground as a blow landed in his stomach. Before he could recover, his attacker was racing away down the street.

'I should have hit him with my handbag,' Snowey said as he watched the retreating figure.

'It's no laughing matter,' Dick Barton announced.

'No sir,' Snowey replied.

'You're going to have to do better than that if we're to stay in business.'

'Yes sir,' said Snowey. He felt suitably chastised.

'Enough said.'

Dick Barton and Snowey turned the corner again and began to walk towards the Riley Monaco which was parked further up the street, where Jock and Lucy, who had come out of the house during the diversion, were waiting for them.

'All well?' Lucy asked as Dick Barton opened the driver's door.

'At least we seem to have shaken him off for the moment,' the special agent replied.

Then, when they were all inside the Riley, Jock turned

from the front seat. 'Give us a kiss then,' he said to Snowey.

'I'm warning you,' Snowey said. 'I'm just in the mood to duff up someone.'

'Now then, now then,' Dick Barton warned.

'Well, I think you're all lovely,' Lucy Cameron put in.

There was laughter as Dick Barton started up the car and began to drive away.

Some hours later, they arrived at the Camerons' neat suburban house on the outskirts of Southampton. Leaving the Riley parked outside the house, Dick Barton and Lucy went in and the others followed. Lucy stopped in the hallway to check the mail. She left the front door open.

'Not a word,' she said as she sorted through the letters.

Then she and Dick Barton went through into the living room. They sat in silence for a while. Jock and Snowey came in.

'All clear?' Dick Barton asked.

'Checked from cellar to attic,' Snowey replied.

'We don't have a cellar,' Lucy put in.

'As clean as a whistle is what he means,' Jock explained.

'Right,' Dick Barton said as he got up from an easy chair. 'We'll go and see what Mr Tibbs has to say for himself. Neither of you leaves here whatever happens.' He turned to Lucy, 'You don't even answer the door.' And then to Jock, 'Let him do it.'

Having delivered his warning, the special agent motioned to Snowey, and they went out of the room together.

'Now I am scared,' Lucy said to Jock.

'Better safe than sorry,' the Scots mechanic remarked. 'The Captain knows what he's doing.'

Lucy Cameron hoped that Jock was right, because if he wasn't, the mystery behind what had happened to her father might never be solved.

In the main laboratory of Merton's, the famous Southampton fertilizer firm, a shaking hand held a visiting card that read: CAPTAIN RICHARD BARTON. The hand belonged to Albert Tibbs, George Cameron's boss. He was nervous that anyone was investigating the disappearance of his colleague. He was speaking into a telephone that he held with his other hand. Behind him, on a range of laboratory benches, stretched rows of glass retorts, phials and other experimental equipment.

'He's here: Barton,' Tibbs said into the telephone. 'Now what do I do? Yes, but you promised me – I wasn't to know. Very well; I'll do what I can.'

When he had finished speaking, he hung up, mopped his brow, then wiped his hand on the sleeve of his white coat. He composed his expression and went over to the internal telephone. 'Ask him to come up,' he said.

When Dick Barton strode into the laboratory he found himself looking at a man who seemed to be just about under control. Not at first sight, he thought to himself, a very villainous-looking villain.

'Mr Tibbs?'

'Captain Barton?'

'Plain mister,' Dick Barton said curtly. 'The war's over. I just haven't got around to getting new cards printed.'

'Quite,' Tibbs replied. He shifted nervously on his feet. 'It's about George Cameron, I understand.'

The special agent came further into the room and began to look around. As far as he could tell there was nothing out of the ordinary. The place was a perfectly normal research laboratory. 'I'm a friend of his daughter,' he said after a while. 'Or rather, a friend of a friend.'

'I feared as much,' Tibbs said. Barton looked questioningly at him. 'It's a distressing business. The child's already spoken to me.'

'Twice,' Dick Barton reminded him. 'On the first occasion you said he'd gone on a business trip.' He paused. 'Then you said he'd left altogether.'

'That's correct.' Tibbs walked over to the nearest bench and began idly running a finger around the rim of a phial.

'I must tell you that the daughter isn't satisfied,' Dick Barton remarked. He didn't like the look of things. He had a feeling that the man was evading something. He wasn't sure what.

'I realise that.'

Dick Barton decided on the direct approach. He had nothing to lose. 'I get the impression that you're hiding something,' he said.

14

'Indeed I am,' Tibbs confessed. 'Whether little Lucy will thank me for revealing it . . . '

'Suppose you let me be the judge of that,' the special agent interrupted.

'As you wish.' Tibbs turned to face Barton again. 'It's a case of *cherchez la femme*.'

'You mean he's simply run off with another woman?'

Tibbs now adopted a portentous manner. He drew himself up to his full height. 'In my experience these things are seldom simple,' he said.

'Yes,' Dick Barton agreed. He took a step nearer the scientist. 'But why would he do that when he's just been reunited with his daughter. Committed himself to them making a life together.'

'I find the war does give some people this heightened sense of melodrama,' Tibbs replied. He wondered whether this fellow called Barton would swallow his explanation. 'Being F.6 myself I was spared it, but I fancy poor George found it hard to adjust to the reality of a humdrum life with humdrum companions.' He paused to find Dick Barton looking at him closely. 'However fond at other levels he may have been of them,' he finished.

'All right,' Barton said tersely. 'But either tell the child or don't. What doesn't make sense is sending her cryptic messages.'

'Messages?' Tibbs said eagerly.

'And why would . . . ' Dick Barton had been going to ask about the banknote. But something in Tibbs's manner persuaded him otherwise.

'Yes?' Tibbs pressed for him to continue.

'Never mind.'

'Who can plumb the workings of the human mind?' Tibbs was now obviously covering something up.

'Who indeed?' Barton played along with the scientist. Then, he asked an unexpected question: 'Do you know the name of the lady concerned?'

Tibbs turned back towards the laboratory bench again. 'I don't really want to make trouble.'

'Don't you think the very least your erstwhile colleague owes his daughter is an explanation?' Dick Barton said firmly. He waited for an answer.

15

In the car park of Merton's, outside the laboratory block, Snowey White stood by the Riley Monaco. He was getting quietly bored out of his mind. He wondered what the governor was up to. So it was with some relief that he greeted Dick Barton when he saw him coming out of the main building.

'Seen him all right?' Snowey asked as he came across to meet the special agent.

Dick Barton nodded. 'And I don't trust him further than I can throw him.'

They began to walk back to the car together. 'What does he say?' Snowey wanted to know.

There was a serious expression on Dick Barton's face. 'That Cameron's gone off with another woman.'

'Well, that doesn't square with the daughter's account,' Snowey put in.

Dick Barton stopped suddenly. 'Right,' he said. 'I'll still have to go and check.' He turned and pointed towards the lab. 'That's Tibbs's boudoir.' He indicated the exact position of the window. 'Stay here and make sure he doesn't leave the place.'

Snowey White shrugged as Dick Barton continued to walk towards the Riley. So he was in for another spot of keeping his eyes peeled. Talk about a lack of excitement. It was worse than the 'phoney war'.

Dick Barton drove the Riley Monaco down a wide street of semi-detached houses. He looked closely at the numbers, checking them as he went. The street was obviously now not of the better sort, though once, he thought, it might have been gracious. He found the number he wanted, stopped the car, and got out. He walked up the garden path and knocked on the door. A middle-aged, rather tired-looking woman answered.

'Mrs Bellows?' asked the special agent.

'That's right.'

'Forgive me for bothering you, but I'm looking for George Cameron, and a colleague of his said you might be able to help.'

The woman looked puzzled. Her brow creased. 'What was the name again?' she said.

'George Cameron,' Dick Barton repeated. 'He's a chemist at Merton's, the fertilizer firm in Southampton.'

'I know them of course,' Mrs Bellows replied. She thought again. 'But George Cameron. No. I'm afraid I can't help.'

'I thought as much,' Dick Barton said grimly. He turned away from the door and began to walk back down the path. 'I'm sorry you've been troubled.'

When the special agent reached the car he started it immediately and drove off fast. It was clear that the address Albert Tibbs had given him had been a false one. He wondered why the scientist had needed a diversion. He hoped Snowey was all right. But most of all he feared for the safety of Lucy Cameron.

Meanwhile, back in the living room of the Cameron home, Lucy was sitting on the sofa, wondering what results would be obtained from Dick Barton's visit to Albert Tibbs. Jock sat across from her in one of the chintz-covered easy chairs.

'I wonder what's keeping your friends,' Lucy said to Jock. But before the Scots mechanic had time to reply the doorbell chimed. 'Speak of the devil,' Lucy added. She began to get up.

'I'll get it,' Jock said firmly. 'Lock the door after me. Don't open it to anyone but me.' He went out into the hall and Lucy locked the living-room door after him.

Jock came out of the living room, and, as he walked down the hall he saw a silhouette through the rippled glass of the front door. He opened the door a chink.

'Yes?'

There was no reply. Instead, the figure hurled his full weight at the door, throwing Jock off balance. The Scotsman tried to counter, but it was too late. The figure moved in on him, and delivered an expert rabbit punch. Jock fell to the ground. Then, the figure beckoned for unseen companions to join him.

Dick Barton reached the fertilizer factory in record time. He screeched the Riley to a halt in the car park in front of the main laboratory building. Then, he got out of the car and ran across to where Snowey White was still keeping vigil.

2 17

'Tibbs still there?' Dick Barton asked.

Snowey pointed up to the window that the special agent had shown him earlier. 'There he is, beavering away.'

Barton looked up, and through the window, could see the dark shadow of a figure with a light behind him. It was indistinct, but Tibbs seemed to be there all right.

'Let's go and find out why he sent me on a wild goose chase,' he said as he walked across in the direction of the main doors. Snowey followed him quickly.

Lucy Cameron thought that Jock was a long time in returning from the hall. She thought she had heard an odd noise, and was listening intently. She heard the sound of feet coming down the passageway and then there was a tap on the door.

'I'm home,' a muffled voice said from the other side of the door.

'Dad!' Lucy cried as she almost jumped out of her chair, and rushed across the room. She quickly unlocked the door and flung it open. But what confronted her was not the benign image of her father returning home. It was something far more sinister. She started to scream. A rough hand was clamped over her mouth and the scream died to a gurgle. Lucy's eyes bulged wide in fear.

The door to Tibbs's laboratory was open. Dick Barton and Snowey burst in and stopped dead in their tracks. For what was sitting in the chair, and had appeared as a shadow from the car park downstairs, was not the true image of Albert Tibbs, but a stuffed dummy sitting up on a bench.

'That's torn it,' Snowey said.

'Lucy!' cried Dick Barton.

Together, they turned and ran out of the laboratory and headed back down the stairs.

Some minutes later, the Riley Monaco again screeched to a halt. But the destination this time was George Cameron's neat suburban house. Dick Barton got out and ran into the house. Snowey followed close at his heels.

It was even worse than they had feared. There was no one in the sitting room, and the once tidy place was now a wreck. The furniture had been upturned, drawers were strewn across the room, and even the curtain rail now stood at a crazy angle. The only neat thing now in the room was an envelope propped on the mantelpiece. Dick Barton's name was typed on the front. The special agent grasped the envelope, ripped it open, and began to read the short, typed message.

'I'll go and check the rest of the house,' Snowey said as he turned on his heel.

'I shouldn't bother,' Dick Barton replied. He began to read the note out aloud, ' "Keep out of this and keep the police out of it if you ever want to see your friend again." ' He paused and turned to Snowey again. 'Unsigned, needless to say,' he added.

Snowey White looked at his governor. They were back in business with a vengeance this time.

Why did Tibbs lie to Barton?
What's happened to Jock and Lucy?
Who wrote the warning note?
Can Snowey and Barton ignore it and save their friend?
Read the next chapter of:
Dick Barton – Special Agent.

Chapter Two

Lucy Cameron's father has disappeared. Someone has tried to stop her going for help. Down in Southampton her father's colleague lied to Barton and vanished, enabling Lucy and Jock to be kidnapped. Barton and Snowey have been warned that if they want to see them again they must drop the case and stay away from the police.

Now read on.

Dick Barton was still studying the mysterious and threatening typewritten message that had been left for him when Snowey came into the living room of the Cameron house. He had been out investigating – on the special agent's orders.

'The neighbours never saw nothing, never heard a dickey-bird,' Snowey exclaimed.

'Wouldn't you know!' the special agent replied. He was trying to think of possible connections. He was worried about the fate of Jock and Lucy.

'Do you think Cameron's mucker snatched Jock and Lucy?' asked Snowey.

Dick Barton looked grave. He put the note back on the mantelpiece. 'I doubt it,' he said. 'He's probably in cahoots with whoever did. Sending me off like that gave them a chance to do their dirty work while he did a bunk. And the whole thing revolves around a rather small firm making fertilizers. That's what beats me.'

Snowey looked around at the wreckage of the once neat room. 'I suppose that is all they do?'

'Good thinking,' Barton replied. He took a step away from the mantelpiece. 'I'll get a line on that. No sense going back to London till we've got this business licked.' Then he came closer to Snowey. 'Besides which it's always possible that Cameron may try to get another message through to Lucy.'

'Now she's been grabbed,' Snowey said flatly.

'He may not know that,' Barton declared.

Snowey looked around the room again. 'So we stop here?'

The special agent nodded. 'Make it our base.' He started to walk towards the door. 'I'll find out what the devil's going on in that firm. You see if you can get sight or sound of our friend Tibbs.'

'Right,' Snowey replied as Barton went out of the room.

The door to the main laboratory in Mertons the fertilizer firm opened, and Tibbs came in beckoning. 'In here, in here,' he said.

Klaus, the man in the leather trenchcoat and trilby, came in followed by three thugs who frogmarched Jock Anderson and Lucy Cameron into the centre of the room.

'I hope you know what you're doing,' Jock said to Tibbs, as at the same time, he struggled against the men who held him.

'I think so,' Tibbs replied confidently. 'Indeed, yes.' There was an evil smile on his face. He indicated the chairs that stood near one of the laboratory benches. 'Kindly secure them.'

The thugs thrust Jock and Lucy on to the chairs, and Klaus produced a piece of rope from his pocket. He then proceeded to tie Jock and Lucy to the chairs.

'Don't struggle or you'll hurt yourselves,' Klaus warned his captives. Then he turned to Tibbs. 'It's a trick I learned in the SS,' he said.

'Remember what happened to Hitler,' Jock Anderson said tersely.

Klaus hit him across the face with the back of his leather-gloved hand. 'Don't be insolent,' the ex-Nazi warned.

'You'll pay for that,' Jock said flatly.

Lucy, who was now bound and tied to the chair by the side of Jock, looked across to where Tibbs was standing. 'And to think you were a friend of Father's,' she said. There was disgust in her voice.

'A colleague. Merely a colleague,' came the reply.

Klaus had now finished his job. It had been well done.

He smiled to himself as he saw Jock Anderson grimace with pain as he tried to move. 'Gag them?' he asked Tibbs.

'Unnecessary,' the scientist replied. 'We had, occasionally, to experiment on animals. Their cries distressed the other staff. So . . . ' He stopped speaking for a moment and walked over to the window. Reaching up, he hauled down a shutter over the window, and secured it at the bottom by turning the key in the lock. Then, across the room, he pulled a heavy steel partition, being careful to leave a gap so that he, Klaus and the thugs could get out. 'When that's closed,' Tibbs continued as he pointed to the partition, 'this end of the laboratory becomes, in effect, a sound-proof box.'

'Where's my father?' Lucy Cameron demanded at that point.

'Yes,' Jock chimed in. 'What have you devils done with George Cameron?'

Klaus looked furious. He wasn't used to having the tables turned on him. 'You ask the questions,' he said to Tibbs.

'Let's be reasonable,' Tibbs replied. 'In any case it'll take me a minute or two to set it up.'

Jock Anderson watched both men closely during the exchange. Tibbs seemed to want to put something off. Jock didn't know what. But his suspicion was confirmed when the man called Klaus spoke again:

'Two minutes. Then, I insist, you proceed as agreed.'

Tibbs then busied himself at his workbench, setting up what appeared to be an experiment. He placed a retort with a red coloured liquid in it over the top of a Bunsen burner. Then he added a structure of glass tubes and condensers to the retort so that its distilled contents would drip on to the protective covering of a large glass jar filled with another substance.

As he worked, Tibbs turned towards Lucy and Jock. 'I'm rather in the hands of other people,' he explained.

Jock gestured to Klaus and his thugs who were lounging against the bench behind Tibbs. 'What do they want?'

'The rest of the formula,' Tibbs replied. He obviously felt it was a simple matter.

'I don't know what you're talking about,' Lucy exclaimed.

'Then why did you get in touch with Barton and co?' came the reply. 'Ah? Ah?'

22

Lucy still didn't quite understand what Tibbs was getting at. 'I got an SOS from Dad,' she replied.

'He was my officer in the war,' Jock Anderson put in.

'An SOS, you say?'

'That's all,' Lucy insisted.

Jock spoke again. 'It's in my wallet if you want to see it,' he said.

There was now a perplexed look on Tibbs's face. He stopped working for a moment. 'I suppose it's possible . . . ' he mused. Then, he appeared to have reached some sort of decision. 'Very well,' he continued. He looked in Lucy's direction. 'Your father was working on a new weed killer. By accident he stumbled upon something with incalculable consequences.' He paused for a moment. 'I was asked to persuade him to part with it.'

'One minute,' Klaus warned ominously from the background.

'Yes, yes,' Tibbs replied placatingly. He turned to Jock and Lucy again. 'He refused,' the scientist continued. 'My principals felt obliged to insist that he helped develop it in their interests. They pointed out that . . . certain people might find themselves at risk unless he agreed.'

Lucy was now beginning to understand what it was all about. 'Me, for instance?' she asked.

'Yes indeed,' Tibbs replied. 'They allowed him to send you money to avert a hue and cry. Then they discovered that his calculations merely produced weed killer.'

The full implications now dawned on Lucy. 'They thought he'd sent me the additional formula,' she said.

Jock Anderson nodded in agreement. Then he looked towards Klaus. 'That's why Fritz here came after you,' he agreed.

'George had it here,' Tibbs said rather desperately. 'I know that for a fact. Somehow he's got rid of it.'

'Time,' Klaus announced. There was no expression in his voice.

'I tell you it's the first we've heard of it,' Jock Anderson said rather desperately. He had no idea what was going to happen to them, but, whatever it was, he was sure that it promised to be nasty.

'That's the absolute truth,' Lucy added.

'Truth is seldom absolute,' the scientist said.

'Enough,' Klaus declared from the background.

Tibbs turned towards Jock and Lucy for the last time. He pointed towards the arrangement of scientific accessories that he had set up on the bench. 'You will find this concentrates the mind wonderfully,' he said. He moved towards it and lit the Bunsen burner. 'This will distill quite quickly. When it has eaten through the protective covering the acid will combine with the contents of the jar to produce a gas which, although lethal, is not, unfortunately, instantaneous.' He then pointed to a small microphone which stood to the right of the apparatus. 'All that you have to do, before you lose consciousness, is to speak into this. I calculate that you have rather less than ten minutes to confide in me. That's if you value your lives.'

When he had finished speaking, Tibbs, accompanied by Klaus and the thugs, went through the gap to the other side of the steel partition and then closed the gap. Lucy looked at Jock Anderson. The mechanic said nothing. The only sound in the now divided room was the bubbling of the retort.

Dick Barton was standing once more in the living room of the Cameron home. He'd just got back from Merton's. He was thinking about the next step when Snowey also arrived back.

'Any joy?' Barton said, as Snowey came into the room.

'Not a sausage,' the ex-sergeant declared. 'It's like he's vanished off the face of the earth.'

Barton began to pace impatiently up and down the room. 'The blasted factory's shut up shop,' he said, 'and I didn't like to be away from here for too long in case Jock or Lucy tried to get in touch.'

Snowey White perched on the arm of an armchair that had been only slightly damaged. 'Now what?' he asked.

The special agent stopped pacing. 'I'll sit tight in case anything breaks,' he declared. 'You get your ear to the ground, find the manager of the factory – he's probably one of Southampton's leading lights.'

'And when I do?'

'Wheel him up here and we'll lean on him a bit,' Dick

Barton finished. He knew that it might not be of immediate help. But, in the circumstances, it was all that they could do. He hoped it was enough.

The slow bubbling of the retort continued. Lucy Cameron was mesmerised by it. She could think of nothing better to do than watch the last ten minutes of her life evaporate slowly away. Then her attention was distracted by a scraping noise. She turned to see Jock Anderson rocking his chair carefully.

'What ... ?' Lucy began.

Jock shook his head, warning her to shut up.

Then, Tibbs's voice came over the two-way receiver. 'Yes,' the scientist said.

'Aren't you afraid someone might come by and wonder what's going on?' Jock asked. As he spoke, he inched his chair slowly towards the laboratory bench, and motioned to Lucy to join in the diversionary chat.

On the other side of the heavy steel partition, Tibbs, Klaus, and the three thugs had made themselves comfortable. They had settled down while they waited for Jock and Lucy to crack.

'Not in the least,' Tibbs replied to Jock's last question.

Then, Lucy's voice came over the speaker. 'You can't be sure of that,' she said.

'We're a very small firm,' Tibbs said. He smiled towards Klaus and the thugs. 'We don't even run to a night watchman.'

While Tibbs and Lucy had been talking Jock had managed to get his chair over to the bench. Now, he inched closer to try and get the rope that secured him to the chair within reach of the flame of the Bunsen burner.

'There's not the slightest chance of anyone disturbing us until the morning,' the scientist's voice continued. 'Which, in your case, will be far too late.'

'Oh . . . ohhh!' Jock burnt himself on the Bunsen, and let out an involuntary yelp of pain which he managed to change into a groan.

'Quite,' Tibbs said over the receiver.

Jock then indicated to Lucy that he wanted her to keep up the chat while he tried again.

'Our friends aren't stupid, you know,' Lucy said to Tibbs.

'Captain Barton and his shadows,' came the reply. 'I should hope not.'

On his side of the partition, Klaus frowned at Tibbs. He was getting impatient. He didn't approve of all the chat. It was a sign of weakness. What he wanted was results.

'Indeed I'm counting on the average ability of your acquaintances,' Tibbs continued. 'Only somebody stupid, or quite exceptionally clever would think of bringing you back to the place from which I fled. If you have any thoughts of being rescued put them out of your mind. This is the last place they'll look.'

'Less talk and more results,' Klaus said to Tibbs as he voiced his impatience.

The scientist spoke into his microphone once more: 'My friends are beginning to get rather restless. You really don't have long, you know. I do urge you to be sensible and co-operate.'

Then, a strange sound come over the microphone. It was a Scottish voice. And what it said sounded remarkably like a muffled, 'Done it!'

'What was that?' Tibbs asked anxiously.

On *his* side of the partition, Jock Anderson had succeeded in freeing himself. When the rope burned through, he pulled the charred remnants off his wrists, switched off the Bunsen burner which had already started the reaction that could have killed both him and Lucy, and moved a glass tube away from the retort. He was just in time; a drop of distilled liquid missed the container that held the substance that would convert into a poisonous gas, and burnt a hole in the floor.

'I said can it!' Jock said into the microphone. He hoped he'd got away with the dodge.

Then, he began to untie Lucy. He spoke into the microphone again. 'It's bad enough being killed without having you bore us to death,' he said to Tibbs. Then, he winked at Lucy.

'I second that,' Lucy added. She winked back at the Scots mechanic.

26

Tibbs's voice came over the receiver once more. 'Brave words. We'll see how brave you are when you get your first whiff of gas.'

Lucy Cameron motioned in Jock's direction. She wanted to know what to do next. But the mechanic wasn't sure. He signalled back that he was still working things out. There was now no immediate rush – he hoped.

By this time, Snowey White, thanks to some impeccable groundwork, had managed to locate the manager of Merton's Fertiliser Factory. Simpson, a large and placid middle-aged man, had now joined them in the living room of the Cameron home. But he was not proving easy to convince. Dick Barton was having trouble persuading him that there might be a major threat to democracy taking place in the medium sized town on the coast.

'Mr Simpson,' the special agent said yet again. 'While we're sitting here the lives of three innocent people are at stake.'

'So help me, he's right,' Snowey White added. He was sitting in one of the replaced armchairs under the window.

Simpson still looked unconvinced. He was impatient, and more than a little angry. 'I'm the manager of a factory making fertilizers in a small way of business,' he replied. 'You interrupt my bridge evening and have me dragged out to the house of one of my research staff to tell me that he has been kidnapped, for no reason that you can suggest. Not only that, but another of them is mixed up in it to the extent of disappearing and arranging for the daughter and a colleague of yours to be kidnapped.' He paused to regain his breath. 'Well . . . I've seen things like it on the films. They don't happen in real life. I can only speak for South-ampton, of course.'

Dick Barton breathed deeply. He was having trouble con-trolling himself. 'You *were* surprised that George Cameron should have gone off like that?' he said to Simpson.

The works manager now had to make some concessions. 'Without a word to anyone?' he replied. 'Yes, I did think that strange. And now you tell me he never even told his daughter . . . ' he paused while he thought for a moment.

27

'Well . . . but that's a far cry from the kind of monkey tricks you're making out.'

Dick Barton turned to look out of the window. All he could see was a neat suburban garden with a lawn and a few dwarf fruit trees. There was nothing that could be called even remotely threatening. But yet he knew that there was something extremely sinister going on. 'All right,' he said after a while. 'I'm short of facts.'

'You said it,' Simpson reminded him.

Snowey White looked up at his governor, then glanced towards Simpson. 'We might find them if you'd let me go in there and take the place apart,' he suggested.

Simpson's reply was adamant. 'I couldn't let you even if I wanted to.'

'Why not?' Dick Barton asked sharply.

'Not without clearing it with Head Office,' the manager explained pedantically.

Barton turned away from the window. It was the same old story, he thought, initiative being stifled by bureaucracy. 'I've spent the last five years, amongst other things, fighting red tape,' he said.

Simpson smiled smugly. 'Yes, I know all about that. Well, the war's over now. You death or glory boys'll just have to learn to settle down a bit.'

'You haven't got a lot to be smug about,' Snowey White chipped in. 'I mean it's a right carry on for a factory, isn't it?'

'There are two opinions about that,' the manager said pompously.

Snowey wasn't going to let him get away with it. 'You must be top of the league for missing scientists this week,' he quipped.

'Tibbs has vanished too,' Dick Barton explained in a more serious tone.

Snowey nodded. 'Houdini couldn't have made a better job of it.'

Barton now sensed that Simpson was wavering. He wondered how long the man could go on ignoring facts that were staring him in the face. 'Forget everything else,' he continued. 'Don't you think Head Office ought to know that two of your staff have gone missing in a week?'

28

'There's something in that,' the manager of Merton's conceded.

'Then why don't you do something about it?' the special agent wanted to know.

'In the morning,' came the reluctant reply.

'The morning might be too late.' Simpson's lack of initiative amazed the ex-captain of commandos.

'I can't call the Chairman, not after office hours,' Simpson explained weakly. 'It's more than my life's worth.'

Dick Barton walked into the middle of the room. 'If I'm right, three other lives may depend on it,' he said grimly. Then, he looked Simpson straight in the eyes.

'I'll tell you what I'll do, I'll call his personal assistant.'

'Help yourself.' Barton pointed to the telephone that Snowey had replaced on an occasional table in the corner of the room.

Slowly, Simpson walked towards the phone. Then, he sat himself down in a nearby chair, took a notebook and pencil out of his inside pocket and his glasses out of another. He began to polish the lenses.

Angrily, Dick Barton watched the manager go through his series of delaying tactics.

'His middle name's not lightning, is it?' Snowey said softly.

Back in the laboratory at Merton's, Jock Anderson had reached a decision. He and Lucy were now quietly moving about, and keeping up a conversation with Tibbs to cover up their actions.

'You know you'll never get away with this,' Jock said as he dismantled the apparatus on the bench.

'What makes you think that?' Tibbs replied.

Lucy was also trying to find a way out of their predicament. She tried the steel shutters and the partition, but they were both securely fastened. She shook her head so that Jock could see.

'All right,' the Scotsman said into the microphone. 'You've got us cold now, but, come the dawn, how are you going to explain away a couple of corpses?'

Jock, when he had finished speaking, motioned to Lucy to help him move a couple of jars of chemicals to the sink.

29

He began to pour the contents of one down the drain.

'Easily enough,' answered the distorted voice of the scientist.

Jock and Lucy carried on working.

Klaus watched impatiently as Tibbs spoke into the microphone yet again. He had never fully trusted the man. He lacked the moral fibre to be completely ruthless in the service of the cause. He would have never got away with it in the SS. He had no discipline. 'When is this gas going to make them see sense,' he asked.

'Any minute now,' Tibbs replied. Then he spoke into the microphone once more. 'We shall, of course, untie the ropes,' he gloated. 'The assumption will be that Lucy brought you here in search of her father.'

Tibbs's voice droned on in the other half of the laboratory, but neither Jock nor Lucy were really listening. They concentrated as Jock emptied yet another jar of chemicals down the sink.

'I left an experiment to run overnight,' Tibbs went on. 'You began to be overcome by the fumes, panicked and shut yourselves in.'

Jock smiled to himself as gouts of foam began to bubble up from the waste pipe. He didn't know much about chemistry, but it looked as if he was getting the reaction he had hoped for. Then, he quickly replaced the plug, and weighted it down with glass jars, and some heavy pieces of equipment. He mimed to Lucy while he worked. He was trying to tell her that the foam would have to find another outlet.

'It will all pass off as a regrettable accident . . . ' Tibbs continued.

Lucy Cameron hoped that the sink plug would stay weighted down. That Jock Anderson was right and Tibbs was wrong. She didn't want to give up. She wanted to find her missing father. Whatever happened.

Tibbs looked at his watch. If his calculations were correct, then it would not be long before the gas would be generated. 'The best lies are always those nearest the truth,' he said into the microphone.

'Supposing we agree to co-operate?' Lucy's voice came over the receiver.

Klaus frowned deeply. He walked over to where Tibbs was standing. 'No bargains,' he said loudly.

'I see,' Lucy replied.

Tibbs looked up at the ex-SS officer who controlled the whole situation. Sometimes, he wished that he hadn't become so deeply involved in the affair. The implications frightened him.

Now Jock Anderson mimed another series of actions. He wanted Lucy to understand, that, with luck, someone would spot the foam coming out of the drainpipe, and raise the alarm. Lucy nodded back at him. Still, Jock kept up the pretence that they were about to meet their end. They could not afford for Tibbs to discover the truth.

'It's heads you win, and tails we lose, is it?' Jock said to the scientist.

'Correct.'

But Jock and Lucy now knew otherwise. They were in with a fighting chance. They hugged each other.

Klaus was still standing over Tibbs. The scientist looked up at the gaunt-faced ex-Nazi. 'You see,' Tibbs explained. 'The gas is beginning to take effect.'

But Klaus was not impressed. He frowned again. What he wanted was results, not promises.

Outside the main laboratory building of Merton's a uniformed police constable was making his nightly patrol. He walked past the factory gates, and checked that they were shut. He glanced into the yard, and then looked again.

He could hardly believe it. There was a huge column of foam writhing across the yard like some fantastic snake. Bubbles of chemical rose into the air. And more was forming before his eyes ...

When Simpson had finished speaking to the personal assistant of the Chairman of Merton fertilizers, he put down the phone and reversed his ponderous ritual with notebook, pen, and glasses. He turned towards Dick Barton and Snowey. 'He'll put it to the Chairman in the morning,' he said.

The special agent paced angrily up and down. 'Is there nothing I can say?'

'No,' Simpson replied flatly.

'Well, that's it and all about it,' Snowey commented.

Then, the telephone rang shrilly. Snowey picked up the receiver. 'Yes,' he said. 'Hang on.' He held the phone out to Simpson. 'It's for you. Your wife.'

'Ah. Excuse me,' Simpson replied as he took the phone. 'You know how it is.'

'No, actually,' said Dick Barton.

Simpson spoke quietly into the phone. 'Yes, dear. What? No, of course. You were quite right.' When he replaced the phone there was a puzzled expression on his face. 'Strange,' he commented. 'The local constable was passing the works on his beat when he saw what appeared to be a column of foam from the laboratory waste.'

Dick Barton allowed himself a slow smile. His suspicions had been correct. 'But the place is closed for the night,' he said to Simpson.

'Exactly.' The manager had no idea about what was happening.

'So?' said Snowey.

'We're off to the races!' the special agent exclaimed. He began to hustle the bewildered Simpson out of the room.

And, on the safe side of the steel partition, Klaus was also on the telephone. His face was white with anger. 'At once,' he shouted into the mouthpiece, then he replaced the receiver with a clatter. Angrily, he turned to Tibbs. 'You idiot! They don't know anything.'

'Who says?'

'Who do you think?' came the reply. The ex-SS officer pointed at the partition. 'Get the girl out. And she'd better be alive, dumkopf!'

Jock and Lucy heard Tibbs fiddle with the lock on the partition door, and stood in position so that when the door opened they would be concealed behind it.

'Where?' Tibbs said as he came into the room.

'Run for it,' Jock told Lucy.

She did as she was told, but got no further than the outer laboratory, where she was stopped by Klaus and the three thugs. In the meantime, Jock had flung back the heavy partition, and Tibbs, caught in the momentum, had fallen to the floor.

Jock paused to recover his breath for the next round, and was delighted to see Dick Barton, Snowey, and a third man burst into the room.

'Let them have it,' Barton cried.

'Yippee!' Jock didn't need telling. He grabbed the thug nearest to him while Snowey was already piling into the others. Laboratory glassware fell to the floor and smashed, even some of the benches got turned over in the struggle that followed.

Simpson watched in astonishment as all hell broke loose. The bill for damages was going to be considerable. Also on the sidelines stood Lucy Cameron. That was her mistake. Quietly, and without fuss, Klaus pinioned her arm behind her back and marched her out of the laboratory.

'Who's going to pay for all this?' Simpson cried.

But the others ignored him as the fight continued. Jock had managed to get Tibbs down on the floor again, and was hitting him in the face with his fist.

'What have you done with my pal?' he said.

'That's right,' Snowey joined in, 'give it to him Jock?'

Suddenly, in the midst of the melée, Dick Barton turned around. 'Where's Lucy?' he shouted.

'Klaus,' Jock replied grimly.

They broke from the struggle, and leaving the three thugs locked in the laboratory, ran down the stairs. But they had forgotten about Tibbs. As they reached the ground floor of the building, and went out into the yard, just in time to see Klaus forcing Lucy into a large car, the scientist dodged past them.

'Take me with you,' Tibbs shouted after Klaus. He ran towards the gates, confident that the car would stop in time.

But Klaus had other ideas. He pressed his foot down hard on the accelerator. Lucy Cameron covered her eyes as the car knocked Tibbs flying and went over the body with a sickening crunch.

'It's not our night,' Snowey said as the car vanished into the distance.

'They've still got George,' Jock remarked.

'They've got Lucy now,' Snowey added.

'And they stop at nothing,' Dick Barton said grimly. He never underestimated the opposition.

Who is Tibbs's ruthless killer?
Where is he taking Lucy?
Who ordered the change of tack?
Read the next chapter of:
Dick Barton – Special Agent.

Chapter Three

Jock and Lucy have been threatened with a lingering death unless they reveal the formula for a discovery her father, missing scientist George Cameron, has stumbled on. They don't know, but manage to alert Barton and Snowey who come to the rescue. In the ensuing fight Lucy is kidnapped and the suspect colleague of Cameron's deliberately run down and killed.

Now read on.

A thin chalk line marked the spot where Tibbs's body had lain. Three policemen clustered around the outline as a large Humber came through the gates of Merton's Fertilizer Factory. The car horn sounded and the driver, a thin faced young man, who was personal assistant to the firm's Chairman, General Edward Wilson, got out and walked around to the passenger side.

'Stand back, stand back,' General Wilson said to Peter Ashe. 'I'm not in my dotage, am I?'

'No, General.'

'Then don't fuss,' Wilson continued as he began to walk across the yard to the laboratory building. 'Just bring any bumph I need.'

It was then that Simpson, the works manager appeared, the swing doors of the laboratory block closed behind him. 'General Wilson . . . ' he began anxiously.

The large, red faced older man came straight to the point. 'Simpson,' he said. 'Let's have it. Right from the shoulder. What kind of a mess have you let us in for, hm?'

The works manager began to explain, but Wilson had already pushed past him, gone through the main doors, and was making his way upstairs towards the first floor laboratory.

Fragments of glass, pieces of shattered equipment, and heaps of assorted chemicals still littered the floor of Tibbs's workplace. After the struggle during which Klaus had escaped with Lucy, no attempt had been made to clear the place up. Dick Barton, Snowey and Jock, stood amid the wreckage, pondering their next move.

'It looks as though the Big White Chief's arrived,' Barton said from near the window.

As if to confirm the special agent's announcement, General Wilson's voice echoed in the outside corridor. 'I can't abide a man who beats about the bush.'

'And how,' Jock Anderson commented.

'Just cut the cackle and get down to cases, there's a good chap,' the loud voice continued as footsteps came nearer.

'Stand by your beds, men,' Snowey White said to the others. Jock smiled back at him.

Then, Wilson, accompanied by Ashe and Simpson, burst into the room. 'Damn mess, isn't it?' he declared immediately.

Flustered, Simpson began to explain: 'I didn't like to get it cleared up in case the police . . . '

'Absolutely not,' the General interrupted. He spoke in short, sharp sentences. 'Accidents happen in the best regulated families. They clear them up. First rule of regimental soldiering. This is nothing to do with the police. It's bad enough having them snooping around that corpse but I do see you might have a job to hush up that sort of thing.'

'It's being treated as a straight case of hit-and-run driving,' Ashe said placatingly.

'Good thinking.' The General turned to Simpson. 'Then there's no reason not to get this place straightened up.'

'I'll see to it, sir,' the works manager replied. He turned to go out of the room.

'And look sharp about it!' Wilson then turned his attention to the three men who stood in front of him. He looked them over quickly. 'Now which one of you's Barton?'

'I am, sir,' the special agent replied.

Ashe held up a buff coloured folder he had been carrying. 'Sir Richard Marley's report,' he said as he held it out for the General to look at.

Wilson ignored the offer. 'I prefer to trust the evidence of my own eyes,' he replied. There was a long pause while he looked Dick Barton up and down. After a while, he appeared to be satisfied with what he saw. 'I like the way you stand over your ground,' he said.

'Thank you, sir.'

The General turned towards Ashe once more. 'Now let's have a look.' This time, he took Sir Richard Marley's account of 'The Great Tobacco Mystery' and gave it a quick look over. 'You see,' he said to Barton. 'I'm seldom wrong. Marley gives you a clean bill of health. Your other ranks too.' He gestured over Barton's shoulder. 'Are these they?'

'04723,' Snowey said, playing the General's game. 'White. George Victor. Sergeant. Late 17 Commando.'

'Known as Snowey, I'll be bound,' Wilson commented.

'Sir!' Snowey came smartly to attention.

'Carry on,' the General said.

Snowey relaxed once more.

'Anderson, Jock. Private.'

'A Jock, eh?' the General burbled on. 'I'm proud to know you. Salt of the earth. I commanded the Highland Division at one time.'

'I was in REME,' Jock said quietly.

'Oh. Well, never mind,' Wilson rambled. 'They also serve who make the wheels go round.'

Snowey looked at Jock, and the Scotsman looked back. They didn't need to say anything.

'Congratulations, Barton,' the General continued. 'A fine body of men. What's the form?'

Ashe took a step forward. 'Well, General. As I was explaining on the way down . . .'

'Yes. Yes,' Wilson said impatiently. 'I don't want all that.' He looked at Dick Barton. 'Be a good chap and give me a sitrep in plain English.'

The special agent glanced at Snowey and Jock. He knew what they were thinking. 'One of your scientists seems to have stumbled on something with "incalculable consequences",' he said to Wilson. 'He was kidnapped. Whoever did it found he'd protected his discovery by concealing part of the formula. They thought he'd sent it to his daughter and Jock here.'

'But he hadn't?'

37

'No.'

'He'd just sent her a coded plea for me to help,' Jock explained.

The General shook his head at the stupidity of others. 'Amazing how people can get hold of the wrong end of the stick, isn't it.' Then, he looked at Barton and saw that the special agent was impatient to get on with his account. 'Still, go on.'

'To cut a very long story short,' Dick Barton said concisely, 'the daughter's now been kidnapped too.'

Wilson nodded sagely. 'There you are, you see,' he said to Ashe. 'Plain as the nose on your face when you take out the trimmings.' He faced the special agent again. 'Well Barton: you seem to have got the situation pretty much in hand. What's the problem?'

Snowey White glanced at Jock again. He raised one eyebrow.

'We need to know what George Cameron discovered.' Barton's tone was short.

Once again, a look of bewilderment crossed the General's face. 'I thought you said . . . '

'We were told it was something "with incalculable consequences",' Jock Anderson interrupted. He was getting tired of waiting for the penny to drop.

'But not what?' Ashe asked suddenly.

'No,' said the special agent.

'Shouldn't you have asked?' the General blustered.

The Scots mechanic took a deep breath. 'Lucy, that's the daughter, and me were about to be gassed at the time.'

A look of anger made Wilson's face seem even redder. 'Disgusting weapon. And in flagrant breach of the Geneva convention,' he commented irrelevantly. Then, he seemed to realise that he had gone off the point. 'Still, we're not much forrarder, are we?'

'We wouldn't be so clueless if we knew what Cameron'd been working on,' Snowey said.

The General turned to Ashe with an expression of surprise. 'Why didn't you think of that?'

'I'll make enquiries,' the assistant said dutifully. Then, he went out of the room.

'Wonderful, isn't it?' the General commented. 'Brains first

38

rate, initiative none. Forever putting the horse before the cart.'

Snowey White then spoke softly to Jock. 'Your pal,' he said. 'I don't give a prayer for George and Lucy's chances if we've got to work through him to get to them.'

The General didn't hear anything. He looked around the room as if he was disgusted that it hadn't been cleaned up yet. Dick Barton walked over to the window once more. He was frowning deeply.

Klaus pushed Lucy Cameron into the room, and then locked the door behind her. It was a fairly large, well furnished space with a settee and two easy chairs. There was no window, but a north facing skylight supplied enough daylight. But, the moment she entered, Lucy was not interested in the incidentals. There was a man sitting slumped over a table under the skylight. She had no trouble in recognising him.

'Dad!'

'Lucy!'

George Cameron rose from where he was sitting. His whole attitude changed. At first he was delighted to see his daughter. But, even as he put his arms around her, disappointment crept into his voice.

'I wanted to keep you out of this,' he said.

Lucy held her father at arm's length so that she could look at him more easily. 'Oh, but it's good to see you again.'

'Couldn't you get to Jock?' the scientist asked soon after. Tension had returned.

'Yes, but someone followed me,' his daughter explained. 'And then Mr Tibbs tried to scare us into telling him the rest of the formula.'

'You didn't know it.'

'They wouldn't believe that,' Lucy replied. She shivered as she remembered the events in the laboratory. 'At least at first . . . then, just when we might have been able to get away . . . I stayed to watch and that man . . . ' she pointed towards the door.

'That's Klaus,' her father explained.

'Klaus grabbed me and . . . ' she almost broke down as she told the story. 'Mr Tibbs wanted to come too.' She couldn't control the shudder this time. 'He simply drove straight over him. It was horrible.'

'My poor darling.' Her father drew her close to him for a moment.

'But you're all right,' Lucy said after a while. 'That's the main thing.'

'Yes,' George Cameron replied, but there was no enthusiasm in his voice. He looked around the room. 'Apart from keeping me here, they really haven't treated me badly.'

Lucy followed her father's glance. On a comfort level, there was really little to complain about, she thought. All that was missing was freedom. 'Who are they?' she wanted to know next.

George Cameron thought for a while. His captors had been careful to conceal their real identity, if not their purpose, from him. 'German, Swiss? I'm not sure?'

'And why?'

The scientist sat down again. What had happened would take quite a lot of explanation. He hoped his daughter would understand. 'I was working on this weedkiller,' he began. Already, images of the past had began to flash through his mind. 'It was nothing special. Then, one day,' he suddenly saw himself that morning in the laboratory standing in front of his bench in his white coat. Still innocent. 'Part accident, part curiosity,' he continued. 'I added . . . ' He couldn't bring himself to tell her the formula. It was too dangerous. 'I found it stopped all forms of life.'

'No!' Lucy exclaimed with horror.

Suddenly, George Cameron felt an enormous release. He simply had to tell someone. 'Not just weeds, plants, trees. But insects, birds,' he went on. 'Every living thing. Quite simply it laid waste to everything.' Even now, he found himself with a ghastly vision of an England that was totally sterile. He gained control of himself and began to speak again. 'And from an amount . . . If my calculations were right just one jar of it could have made the whole country barren. And forever. There was no way of reversing the process that I could see.'

'Oh, Dad.' Lucy suddenly felt an enormous pity for her father. That his profession should have led him to such a monstrosity.

40

'I must have blurted out something to Albert Tibbs,' the scientist explained. 'I didn't know what to do . . . ' He covered his face with his hands again. 'If it fell into the wrong hands . . . I split the formula. I wrote to our Chairman to tell him what I'd found. He didn't even bother to reply.' He looked up at his daughter again. 'Then, one day, Tibbs asked me to meet some friends of his.'

'Foreigners?'

'That's what decided me,' Cameron replied. 'They knew all about it.'

Lucy moved closer to her father. She now understood the enormous weight of the responsibility he had been carrying. It explained all the small things, the lapses in his daily routine that had been worrying her before his disappearance, though she had never said anything to anyone. 'But how could they?' she asked.

The scientist shook his head. 'I don't know. They offered to pay huge sums. Only . . . with that, you could hold the world to ransom, do you see? When I refused . . . I wanted to keep you out of it.' At this point George Cameron got up from the table, and began to walk about. 'I thought at least Jock would take care of you,' he explained. He stood dejectedly in the centre of the room. 'And now . . . '

Lucy also got up and walked over to her father. She placed a hand on his arm. 'It's all right. It's all right,' she said quietly.

'How can you say that?' came the distraught reply. 'These people'll stop at nothing. Now they got you . . . '

'Jock and his friends are still free,' Lucy said. She hoped that, even now, they were working on the release of her father and herself.

But, in spite of Lucy Cameron's hopes, progress in a solution to the affair was still going only slowly. Back in the laboratory at Merton's, Dick Barton, Snowey and Jock stood in a half circle around General Wilson and his personal assistant. Ashe had just come back into the room after doing some checking. In the background, cleaners were at work cleaning up the debris left after the fracas with Klaus, Tibbs and company.

'According to the records,' the pale faced young man

declared, 'Cameron and Tibbs were working on the development of a new weed killer.'

The General huffed quietly. 'Useful. Competitive even, in this day and age,' he remarked. 'But hardly the thing to go to war for, would you say?'

'If that was all,' Dick Barton cut in sharply.

Jock picked up the point. 'We were told that George had stumbled on to something "with incalculable consequences".'

'That's right,' Snowey agreed.

'If you heard aright,' Ashe commented. His manner was stiff and unfriendly.

'What're you trying to make out?' the Scotsman demanded.

'You and the girl were under threat – ' Ashe reminded him.

Jock was furious. He wasn't going to have his integrity questioned by some jumped-up pipsqueak of a personal assistant. 'I'm telling you what was said!' he insisted.

'Keep your hair on, my old china,' Snowey said.

'Let's go at it another way,' Dick Barton suggested. He didn't like the look of Ashe, and would trust Jock Anderson before an army of pen pushers any time. But this was an occasion that called for diplomacy. 'Have you had any outside moves to suggest that there might be more to this company than meets the eye?' he asked.

'Good point,' General Wilson conceded. He looked to Ashe for confirmation. 'There was that Swiss bid, wasn't there?'

'Swiss bid, sir?' the personal assistant looked blankly at his superior.

'Don't tell me you've forgotten?' Wilson said impatiently. As always when he became irritated, his face became a deeper shade of red. 'You were keen enough at the time.'

'Oh, the Swiss bid,' Ashe covered. 'I just thought it was generous.'

'Too generous by half,' the General declared to Dick Barton. 'I smelt a rat at once. Anyway I hate the Swiss.' He paused, but since no one took him up on the point, he had to explain further. 'Well, how long since they've been in a scrap, eh? Only fit for chocolate and cheese with holes in it. Beside, I took against the fellow. Forget his name. We turned him down flat, didn't we?'

'You did,' Ashe replied.

'Suppose they knew what Cameron was on to?' Dick Barton suggested. 'What would they need to develop it themselves?'

Wilson looked puzzled for a moment. 'Ah,' he said eventually. 'I follow. You mean in terms of premises. Facilities. Beyond me, I'm afraid.'

The cleaners had now nearly finished. A semblance of order had been restored to Tibbs's laboratory. Dick Barton watched as piles of glass fragments were placed in cardboard boxes and carried out. 'It'd have to be somewhere fairly big to develop and test a chemical product.'

'Quiet enough not to upset the neighbours,' Snowey added.

'And near enough for them to do all that to-ing and fro-ing with me and Lucy,' Jock finished.

The special agent turned to his friends. 'That narrows the field a bit, doesn't it?'

'Do the round of the house agents?' Jock suggested.

Dick Barton nodded. He was relieved that they were getting back into action. Standing around chatting to old military gentlemen whose idea of a campaign was still trench warfare wasn't exactly his way of conducting an investigation. 'Find out whether any foreigners have taken a place that might fit the bill within a radius of twenty miles, say,' he said to Jock and Snowey.

'Right away.' Snowey motioned to Jock and they both moved towards the door. They smiled at each other as they went.

'Capital,' Wilson said as they went out. 'A first rate appreciation, Barton. They're to have any assistance they require, Ashe.'

'General.'

The older man turned to his assistant again. 'Meantime . . . I don't know about you but I'm as hungry as a hunter. Let's go and have a bit of lunch, shall we?'

The door to the room in which George Cameron was being kept prisoner opened, and Klaus, accompanied by three thugs, came in carrying plates, cutlery and a large picnic

43

hamper. They began to lay the table with over-elaborate politeness. The scientist noticed that three places were being prepared, and that the meal promised to be far more sumptuous than he was used to.

'Who's joining us?' he asked.

Klaus bowed. 'The Herr Professor wishes to make your acquaintance.'

'He doesn't seem to have heard of rationing, does he?' Lucy remarked.

Klauss sniffed. 'The Herr Professor doesn't live by the rules which govern the herd,' he remarked.

Then the door opened again, and Professor Gustave Muller himself entered. He was a smooth, well dressed kind of arch villain, who obviously believed in the good things of life, George Cameron thought. Muller was about fifty, he had a silver grey goatee, and an air of being well fed.

'My dear Klaus,' Muller said as he came into the room. 'You must learn to resist the temptation of making extravagant claims for me.'

The former SS officer bowed, clicked his heels, and said, 'Herr Professor.' Then he went out of the room. The thugs followed him.

'One might be more flattered if one didn't realise he did it to boost his own status,' Muller said to no one in particular. Then he spoke more directly to the imprisoned scientist. 'Permit me to introduce myself, Mr Cameron. Gustave Muller.' He turned in Lucy's direction and smiled. 'And this must be your daughter. Delightful.'

George Cameron took a step towards the smooth-talking villain. 'Did you have her brought here?'

'Yes, I must acknowledge responsibility. In fact for both of you being here.'

'Why?' Lucy wanted to know.

Muller smiled again. Then, he stroked the edge of his beard. 'All in good time, my dear. All in good time. I hate to mix business with pleasure. Let's enjoy our meal first, shall we?' He took a step towards the table. 'A cold collation, but not, I trust, entirely without merit.' He motioned for the scientist and his daughter to sit down. 'Please.'

There was really no option. Lucy and her father sat down as requested.

Snowey White had a grin on his face. He came out of the house agents clutching a mimeographed circular which just might reveal the whereabouts of the people who wanted to get hold of George Cameron's fatal discovery. He nearly bumped into a man who had been following him but who now tried to pass the meeting off as an accident. It was General Wilson's pale faced assistant, Peter Ashe.

'Hello there,' Snowey said.

'Why, hello.'

'Snowey White,' the ex-sergeant introduced himself.

'Of course.' Suddenly, Ashe seemed to remember. 'Mr Barton's right hand man.'

'As of now,' Snowey grinned again. 'Stand on me.'

'You seem very pleased with life,' Ashe remarked.

'I should cocoa.' Snowey held up the mimeographed sheet for Ashe to look at. 'I reckon I've found the house.'

Ashe seemed pleased and surprised. 'Why, that is good news. Come and have a drink.'

Snowey looked around the street. 'I must ring the guv'nor.'

'You can ring him from the pub,' Ashe suggested.

'Why not, eh?'

'Splendid,' the personal assistant smiled again. Then, he took Snowey's arm and led him down the street. Dick Barton's right hand man went along unsuspectingly. He had no idea what lay in store for him.

In the room with the skylight, Muller was just finishing his lunch. He wiped his lips with a table napkin, and reached for the bottle of wine again. Across the table, George Cameron felt uneasy. He had eaten little. Lucy had fewer scruples, she found the sight of such a feast too tempting.

'A touch more Mont Blanc?' Muller said to Lucy as he held out the wine bottle.

'I shouldn't.'

'Indulge yourself,' the reply was accompanied by a well-oiled smile.

'Oh, all right,' Lucy said.

Muller poured wine into the girl's glass. 'One of the beauties of being Swiss is that one enjoys the best of French and Italian cuisine,' the cultivated villain remarked. 'Indeed, German, such as it is.'

George Cameron was a little alarmed by the way Lucy seemed to be on the verge of falling for the civilised charms of the man sitting across the table from him. 'What do you want with Lucy?' he asked suddenly.

Muller looked in the scientist's direction. 'A little feminine guile, that's all.'

Lucy looked questioningly over the rim of her wine glass.

'To persuade your father that he's being very short-sighted,' Muller continued. 'The fact is, while one can delay it, one can't stop progress.'

'It depends what you mean by progress,' George Cameron said. He frowned deeply.

'To be specific,' Muller's voice lost none of its suaveness. 'Someone else is going to discover your discovery one day.'

George Cameron pushed his plate away. 'By then there may be safeguards for it.'

'Must you take the world on your shoulders?' Muller asked.

The scientist showed his mounting anger for the first time. 'To protect it from people like you ... '

'Don't be arrogant,' Muller interrupted. The anger in his voice more than matched that of George Cameron. 'I'm a member of the human race aren't I? Do you think, little man, just because I lack your scientific pretensions, I would turn this world into another dust bowl spinning around the sun? What would be the point of that?' He paused for a moment to collect himself. 'You insult my intelligence,' he said more softly. 'What would be the value of that to me?'

Lucy put down her wineglass. She couldn't finish the Mont Blanc now. 'Then why do you want Dad's formula at all?' she asked.

Muller smiled knowingly. 'Because the mere threat of that would be enough to make us rich beyond the dreams of avarice,' he replied as Lucy glanced at him with an unspoken question. 'Yes, us, my child. Your father, you and me.'

The scientist looked hard at Muller. Nothing about the man's intentions pleased him at all. 'I may not amount to very much,' he declared, 'but I've just been through five years of war to keep the world free. I'd never let one nation, let alone one man, hold it up to ransom.' He saw that across the table, his daughter was watching him closely. 'Not with a discovery of mine. Not while there's breath in my body.'

Muller began to rise from the table. 'Perhaps if I were to leave you alone,' he suggested.

Lucy Cameron was furious. She had drunk the Herr Professor's wine, even eaten his food, but she wasn't swallowing his principles. 'You're wasting your time,' she said. 'As it happens I agree with him. Even if I didn't . . . he's my Dad and you heard what he said.'

Muller reached for a small hand bell on the table. 'That makes me very sad,' he said as it tinkled gently.

Klaus soon appeared in response to the signal. 'Herr Professor?'

'Be so good as to bring me the file of photographs on my desk,' Muller ordered.

Klaus bowed and disappeared into the next room.

Muller then reached into his inside pocket and produced a handsome gold cigar case. He opened it slowly. 'A cigar?' he said as he offered the case to Cameron. The scientist shook his head. The over-civilised Swiss criminal then brought out a matching cigar cutter. Slowly, he snipped the end of his cigar, and then lit it with scrupulous care. 'You don't mind if I indulge?' he said to Lucy.

Even as she shook her head Lucy was beginning to dislike the man intensely. But, while he held her father captive, she was going to have to try to placate him. She might even have to do whatever villainy he asked of her.

Now that the laboratory had been cleaned up, Dick Barton was going briskly through the files in the hope of uncovering further information on the weedkiller-turned-total-exterminator that George Cameron had been working on. He hadn't been having much luck. All he had turned up was the routine day by day records of work on fertilizers and related subjects.

'Getting all the help you want?' General Wilson said as he came into the room.

'Thank you, sir,' the special agent replied. 'Unfortunately I don't seem to be making too much headway.'

'Never mind. There's no fire without smoke.'

Jock Anderson then entered. He had a despondent expression, and shook his head as Barton asked, 'Any luck?'

'Not a sausage,' Jock replied. He didn't mention all the places he'd been on his search. What mattered was results – or the lack of them.

'Never say die, eh?' Wilson remarked. 'Maybe the other fellow's doing better.'

'Snowey?' Barton asked.

Jock shook his head once more. 'He'd have a job to do worse.' He walked over to where the special agent was going through the files.

They reeled along the Southampton streets together. They had been from pub to pub, and a casual passerby might have taken them for bosom pals. Only Ashe knew differently. As Snowey White reeled along in front of him, the General's personal assistant permitted himself a slight smile.

'Roll me over, in the clover,' Snowey sang drunkenly as Ashe caught up with him again. He put his arm round his new-found friend. 'You're a bit of a lad, aren't you,' he said.

'Two of a kind,' Ashe replied. His speech was less thick and slurred than the ex-sergeant's. 'What're we celebrating?'

'Haven't a clue,' Snowey said. He seemed to have forgotten the mimeographed sheet of paper in his pocket that might offer a lead on the location of the people behind Lucy's and George Cameron's disappearance.

Ashe produced a small flat bottle from his inside pocket. 'Let's drink to that,' he said, as he offered it to Snowey.

Dick Barton's right hand man guzzled the contents greedily. 'Like I said,' he remarked to Ashe between swallows. 'You're a bit of a lad on the quiet. Does the General know about you?'

'I hope not.'

Snowey laughed. 'You hope not.' He nearly lurched into the gutter and had some trouble righting himself. Ashe helped.

'Let's drink to that,' suggested the personal assistant.

'Right.' There was a longish pause as Snowey emptied the contents of the bottle. 'What is this?' he said when he had finished.

'Scottish wine.'

'Tastes dodgy to me.'

48

'Black market,' Ashe said as he steered Snowey round a corner.

'Aren't you the lad?' Snowey replied. He leaned more heavily on his companion. A thought struck him. He stopped for a moment. 'I've got to ring the guv'nor, haven't I?'

'What about?' Ashe asked innocently.

'Damned if I can remember,' came the reply.

'That definitely deserves another drink,' Ashe suggested.

Snowey raised the bottle to his lips again, and sucked hard at the dregs. 'Definitely.' It was then that he realised that the liquid in the bottle was not ordinary spirits. 'What is this you've been pumping into me?' he asked.

But it was already too late; his eyes glazed over, there was a funny buzzing in his head, and his knees buckled under him. He went down like a poleaxed ox in an anaesthetic parlour.

Ashe looked around quickly. There was an entrance to a warehouse nearby. He dragged Snowey towards it, and dumped him in the doorway. Then, he rifled through his victim's pockets, and found the mimeographed sheet. He seemed pleased with himself.

The moments passed in the room with no windows. Muller seemed to be entirely absorbed in his cigar. He drew on it slowly, inspecting the end from time to time.

The tension rose between Lucy and her father. They wondered what he was planning. They glanced worriedly at each other and then looked towards their captor.

The sleek, civilised Swiss returned their glances. His eyes were clear, and he looked contented. But when he smiled it was with a look of such pure, undiluted evil that Lucy found herself shivering. She daren't even look at her father.

Jock looked across to Dick Barton, and it was the special agent's turn to shake his head. They had come up with nothing but harmless chemical formulas and routine results for the past half hour. Wilson was standing behind them. One of the laboratory benches was littered with files.

'It looks like we've run into a brick wall,' Jock finally admitted.

Wilson nodded sympathetically. 'Sergeant White didn't

strike me as the kind of chap to let a little difficulty get in his way.'

Jock and Barton exchanged glances. Neither of them had mentioned Snowey. It was unlike him not to make contact at least.

'Let's hope he's getting somewhere,' Barton said slowly. He meant it.

But in the warehouse doorway, near the docks, Snowey White was in no condition to be getting anywhere at all. If he was conscious, he would have known that his body was being covered with rough sacks. But he wasn't.

The pale-faced young man called Ashe was satisfied with his work. He took a last glance at his victim, and then walked over to the side of the dock. He threw the small, flat, incriminating bottle into the water. It sank slowly out of sight as he walked quickly away.

What new devilry is Muller planning?
Is Snowey drunk?
Or drugged? Or dead?
Read the next chapter of:
Dick Barton – Special Agent.

Chapter Four

Professor Gustave Muller, in his attempt to get his hands on the lethal life-destroying formula accidentally invented by George Cameron, threatens something fiendish unless Lucy and her father co-operate. Meanwhile, Dick Barton and Jock Anderson have come to a dead end in their investigations. Unknown to them, Snowey White has been drugged or murdered by General Wilson's personal assistant, Peter Ashe.

Now read on.

He opened his eyes very slowly but closed them again immediately. The light was too bright, and there was something funny about it. It was coming through the small square holes of a loosely-woven material. Snowey White had a headache and his throat was feeling dry. He threw aside the pile of sacks that covered him, and blinked again. His hand went to his inside pocket. It didn't take him long to discover that the particulars of the house were missing.

'Streuth!'

He looked at his watch and saw that it was late. But he still might just make it in time. He started to run down the waterside. With every step his head hurt even more.

About a quarter of an hour later, Snowey reached the entrance to the house agent's where he had previously met Ashe. But, this time the circumstances were different; there was no personal assistant and it didn't look as if there was anyone inside the office either. There was a small cardboard sign reading 'CLOSED' hanging on the door.

He rang the bell twice and hammered loudly on the door with his fist. There was no reply. Slowly, it began to dawn on him that there was no option but to return to the guv'nor, and tell him that he had lost what was probably their only lead. And he'd got drunk into the bargain. He didn't relish the prospect.

'Oh, blimey, O'Reilly,' Snowey said out loud. He turned and began to walk back down the street.

When Klaus returned to the room in which George Cameron and Lucy were being held prisoner, he was carrying a large folder. He handed it to Gustave Muller, and then stood waiting for further instructions.

'Thank you,' the Swiss replied. 'You may leave the room.'

As Klaus turned and went out again, Muller looked closely at the contents of the folder. He spent some time peering at the large photographs.

'As a scientist,' he said to George Cameron after a while, 'you'll be familiar with the system of rewards and punishments.' He turned to Lucy, 'Popularly known as the carrot and stick principle.' Then he turned back to Cameron again. 'So far I have been offering you rewards.'

'Nothing you can do will make me change my mind,' the scientist replied.

Muller leant back in his chair. 'That's probably true,' he said thoughtfully. 'Through the ages martyrs have been made of the most unpromising material. However, you may be less sanguine about the stick being meted out to Lucy.'

'You can't frighten me either,' Lucy declared.

Muller looked down and then at his prisoners. 'I should tell you I'm a professor of psychology. As such I'm interested in the equations we have to make,' he paused and an evil smile crossed his face. 'For instance, your integrity plus . . . what? equals this really enchanting creature. Your own child,' he continued slowly. 'Your only child.'

Lucy could see that Muller's veiled threats were beginning to get through to her father. 'Don't listen to him,' she said.

'What are you suggesting?' George Cameron asked his captor.

'I have recently acquired the services of a surgeon who experimented in the camps,' Muller replied. He saw the sudden look of fear in Lucy's eyes. 'Yes, my dear,' he added, 'those camps.' He looked towards the scientist again; 'I can't claim that the results were rewarding therapeutically,' he

52

said, 'but they were . . . interesting. Very.' Then, with a sudden movement, he held up the horrific photographs for Lucy and her father to see.

Lucy caught a quick glimpse and then shut her eyes. She had heard enough about the terrible mutilations carried on in the camps under the name of research. She didn't need a visual reminder of the outrages carried out by so-called scientists. 'Don't look!' she exclaimed to her father.

'Yes, look,' Muller urged in a voice as soft as crushed velvet. 'You won't sell your principles. Very well. Is the price you put on them high enough to see your child turned into a monstrosity?'

When Lucy opened her eyes again the photographs were still being held up. She turned her head away. It was not possible . . .

Then, the door opened and Klaus marched in suddenly.

'Now what is it?' Muller asked. He was furious that the tension had been broken at a crucial moment.

Klaus handed him a written message.

'Very well,' Muller said to his German assistant. 'You must excuse me a moment,' he said with mocking politeness to his captives. He pointed to the photographs before going out of the room. 'Think about them,' he said. 'You know the alternatives.'

When Muller had gone, Lucy looked at her father. His face was grey, and the veins stood out on his forehead. She could see that he was wrestling with his conscience. He looked down at the photographs and then at his daughter. Their eyes could not meet. They looked away from each other.

Snowey White had returned to Merton's laboratory. He stood looking at the floor while his governor berated him for his careless conduct. And, if that wasn't bad enough, General Wilson and Jock were also present. Snowey felt about as low as a grass snake at the bottom of a lift shaft.

'Anything to say for yourself?' Dick Barton said, after his initial anger had abated.

'It hasn't happened since the night we crossed the Arno,' Snowey offered.

'It doesn't matter how often it happens,' the special agent

53

replied. 'The point is that you've let the side down, and dashed badly.'

'I'm very sorry, sir.'

'If it happens again you'll find yourself looking for another billet. Clear?'

'Sir!'

Barton then softened. Telling Snowey off wasn't something that he particularly enjoyed doing. But the point had to be made. 'Very well,' he finished, 'we'll say no more about it.'

'Capital, Barton,' Wilson huffed from the background. 'Just how I used to be. Give them hell and make an end of it. Only way.'

Jock, who had been glad when the ticking off ended, now turned sympathetically to Snowey. 'What got into you?' he asked.

Snowey answered quietly, 'I reckon Mr Ashe slipped me a mickey finn.'

But, apparently, he was not quite quiet enough. The remark was overheard by the General. 'My personal assistant?' Wilson demanded.

'Why should he?' Barton said curtly.

Snowey looked from one to the other. He didn't know anything about motivation and all that rubbish. All he knew about was what happened.

'He gave me this half of bitter and that was it. Curtains,' he explained.

Barton turned to General Wilson. 'Perhaps we should get him in and see what he has to say.'

'I should hope so, too,' Wilson replied. 'Hang it all,' he glanced reproachfully at Snowey, 'give a dog a bad name and some of the mud sticks . . . I know what I mean,' he blustered, 'and, frankly, White, I'm surprised at you. But I'll have the fellow here in two ticks and we'll see.' Then, obviously in a temper, the General stormed out of the room.

'You'd better be right,' Jock warned Snowey. 'Or there'll be hell to pay.'

George Cameron and his daughter sat at either side of the table in the room with no windows. The photographs lay between them. They hadn't spoken since Muller had gone out. There seemed to be nothing to say. Then quietly, and without sobbing, Lucy began to cry.

'It's all right, my darling,' the scientist said comfortingly. 'I won't let it happen to you.'

'I'm sorry,' Lucy wiped her eyes with her handkerchief. 'I did mean to be so brave. But ... '

George Cameron glanced once more at the photographs. 'I know. It's all right.'

'It isn't!' Lucy insisted.

'I promise you ... ' her father began.

'When you've tried so hard,' came the reply.

The scientist pointed towards the photographs. 'Nothing's worth letting that happen to you.'

Ashe had returned to the main laboratory when the General had asked him to. He was having a hard time of it in front of Dick Barton and his company. At first, they didn't seem to be convinced by his explanation.

'So much for being a good Samaritan,' he replied bitterly when taxed with the suggestion that he had slipped Snowey a mickey finn.

'Come again?' Snowey replied.

'You don't deny drinking with Snowey?' the special agent cut in.

'Certainly not.' Ashe was adamant. He looked to the General for support. That was one old buffer who was easy to convince.

'Fair, square and above board, you see,' Wilson remarked.

Encouraged now, Ashe continued with his duplicity. 'I offered to buy him a drink,' he said, indicating Snowey, 'before I realised he was in a filthy state already.'

Snowey couldn't believe his ears. 'A what?' he said. 'I hadn't had a drink all day.' He looked at his guv'nor, then at Wilson. Then, last of all, at Ashe. 'I tell you,' he insisted.

When Snowey White looked at him Ashe knew that all that he could do was to carry on lying. It was touch and go whether he was going to make it. 'He was falling about the place,' he alleged, 'and waving the particulars of this house, the discovery of which he was apparently celebrating. When he collapsed, I left him to sleep it off.'

'You came down the docks,' Snowey countered. 'Knees

up, singing and the rest, and drinking drink for drink with me!'

Ashe looked coldly at his former drinking companion. 'You were singing,' he said. 'I was trying to get the bottle away from you.'

'You did collapse?' Dick Barton asked Snowey. He wanted a straight answer.

'Well, yes,' Snowey admitted. It was the truth wasn't it. But it wasn't because he couldn't hold his beer. He wished they'd believe him.

'Why didn't you tell us then?' Jock asked Ashe sharply.

The personal assistant gave the Scotsman a bland look. 'Frankly, it never occurred to me.'

General Wilson, who had been waiting to say something for a while, now blustered in in his usual fashion. 'Nor should it,' he said as he defended his employee. 'Sneak on some unfortunate to his CO? I'd have kicked his bottom if he had, I tell you.'

Barton was still not sure that he totally trusted Ashe. There was something about the pale-faced young man's manner that he hadn't liked from the start. 'You could have given us the particulars of the house,' he said succinctly.

It was Barton that Ashe feared the most. Sometimes, the man's sheer intelligence threatened to expose the whole charade. 'Without disclosing how I came by them?' he tried. He looked to his employer for support. 'Hardly. Naturally I took care of them, hoping to return them in such a way as to enable Mr White to cover his lapse.'

'And how do you repay him?' Wilson angrily asked Snowey. 'Answer me that? With slander and back-biting and a pack of snivelling lies.'

Ashe seized his moment. 'As it is,' he said, as he reached into his pocket and produced the mimeographed sheet he had earlier taken from Snowey. He handed it to Dick Barton.

'It seems you owe Mr Ashe an apology,' Barton said to Snowey as he took the information that Ashe offered him. The special agent still wasn't completely convinced. But, he thought for the moment, the best thing to do was to play along.

'Oh please.' The personal assistant waved his hands in the

air. ' "Wine is a mocker and strong drink is raging." ' He turned to Snowey, 'I've no hard feelings.'

'There,' General Wilson commented. 'Nobody could say fairer than that.' He slapped his assistant on the back. 'Handsome my boy. Handsome, indeed.'

Snowey didn't like it at all. He didn't know what Ashe was up to, but it must be something pretty fishy, he thought. He'd better keep an eye on him in he future. 'Sir – ' he began.

'Skip it,' Dick Barton replied tersely. He was looking closely at the information he had obtained too late. 'The description seems to fit the bill,' he remarked. 'Let's see if we can find the place on the map, shall we?'

Jock Anderson brought the map of the area out of his pocket and unfolded it on the bench in front of them. Immediately, he and Dick Barton began to trace the site. Disgruntled, Snowey joined them a moment later.

'Shall we be returning to London, General?' Ashe asked his employer as he saw the Dick Barton company busy themselves.

'Not until we get this business sorted out.'

'I'll inform Head Office, if you'll excuse me.' Ashe started to walk towards the door. As soon as his back was turned he permitted himself a slight smile. The ruse had worked. He wondered if Barton knew what he was letting himself in for.

When Gustave Muller came into the room again, he looked gloatingly at George Cameron and his daughter. 'Do I detect a change of ethical atmosphere?' he said.

The scientist looked at the so-called Professor of Psychology with hatred. 'You filthy swine,' he replied.

Muller shrugged urbanely. 'Words. Words.'

'You know I can't let you do that to her.'

'I'm glad,' Muller commented as he came further into the room.

Lucy stood up. She'd wiped the tears from her eyes but her face was still strained and pale. 'Well, I'm ashamed,' she said, 'and you've probably broken Dad's heart.'

The Swiss shrugged. 'Hearts break in books, my dear. In life, you'll learn, they merely ache.'

George Cameron looked up at the man who held them

57

both prisoner. 'Let her go,' he pleaded.

'Where's the rest of the formula?'

'In the frame of a photograph Jock and I had taken in Hamburg,' the scientist replied.

'The one in the living room?' Lucy put in.

He nodded at his daughter. There was a faraway look in his eyes. 'I had a crazed sort of hope that if you got to him, he might . . .'

'Splendid,' Muller interrupted. He looked pleased with himself. He stroked his beard.

'Now let her go.'

Muller came over to the table. 'When we have it – and are confident that, this time, it works – I shall be more than happy to let you both go.'

Despite herself, Lucy found her interest quicken at the mention of freedom. 'When will that be?' she said.

'Ah,' came the reply. 'To tell you the truth I'm a little preoccupied with disposing of your bothersome friends at the moment. Barton and co.,' he elaborated when Lucy looked questioningly at him. 'But that shouldn't exert us overlong or unduly.' He reached down to pick up the photographs. 'Shall I?' he said to himself. 'No, on second thoughts . . . ' he replaced them on the table. 'If I leave them with you,' Muller finished, 'they will discourage any belated tendency towards heroism to which you might otherwise fall prey.' And with that, the psychologist with the gentleman's manners, but the mind of an evil criminal genius, left the room.

When the key once more turned in the lock, and they were alone with a folder full of crimes against humanity on the table in front of them, Lucy turned to her father:

'Now we don't have any cards left to play,' she said.

The scientist, though, had not yet given up the game. 'As a matter of fact,' he began.

'Yes?' Lucy replied, hopefully.

'There is a third part to the formula.'

'Where?'

'It's better that you shouldn't know,' George Cameron said seriously.

'But, Dad,' Lucy answered. She was beginning to feel afraid again. 'When they find out it still doesn't work . . . '

her voice trailed off at the unmentionable consequences.

'We'll have won time,' her father said with more confidence. 'If we're lucky, time enough for Jock and his pals to get here.'

When he had spoken, they looked at each other for a long time. There was nothing more to be said.

As he, Dick Barton, and Jock looked over the map together, Snowey felt some of the old comradeship come back. They obviously weren't that cheesed off with him then. Still, he was going to have to make up for his bloomer somehow. He concentrated on the area of the map immediately surrounding the house. 'Lumme,' he remarked after a while. 'We're going to have our work cut out to get near there without being spotted.'

'There doesn't look to be a lot of cover,' Jock Anderson agreed.

'Stretch of dead ground here,' Dick Barton pointed to the exact spot.

'If you want my advice . . . ' General Wilson chimed in from the background. But he stopped when the special agent stared coldly at him. 'Quite right,' he said, covering his embarrassment. 'Terrible habit that, sticking one's oar in. Too many cooks only ship water. I won't say another word.'

'As soon as it's dark,' Dick Barton said to the others, 'I'll do a recce.'

'Why waste time?' Jock suggested. 'They could be doing anything to George and Lucy.'

'Jock's right,' Snowey agreed. He remembered the sickening crunch as that Kraut feller had driven straight over Albert Tibbs. 'We're up against a diabolical crowd.'

'All the more reason not to go off at half cock,' Barton insisted. 'You go back to base. Get some rest. Soon as I've had a shufti I'll join you. We'll work out a joint plan of attack.' He turned to Snowey in particular. 'I want you fresh and fighting fit by then,' he continued. 'And you're on no account to leave base, either of you, until you hear from me.' He began to fold the map up again. 'That's an order.'

Snowey White looked at Jock and shrugged. There was no arguing with the guv'nor, that was obvious. Not after the mess he'd got himself in with Ashe.

The scientist and his daughter held hands in their comfortable prison. The moments ticked by too slowly. There was no sound from outside, not even the distant roar of traffic. There were no distractions at all from the terrible fate that awaited Lucy if they did not obey Muller's instructions.

It was a question of hope that Dick Barton and his friends would arrive in time. Lucy gripped harder.

The Riley Monaco stopped on the winding country road. Dick Barton cut the engine, and switched off the lights. He had just gone past the drive of the country house whose address he had obtained from the mimeographed sheet given him by Ashe. He got out of the car. His face was blackened with burnt cork, and he was wearing a camouflage jacket and a woolly commando hat pulled low over his forehead. He went around to the back of the car and produced a camouflage net from the boot. He draped it over the Riley. Then, after looking around to make sure that he had not been seen, he began to work his way back towards the drive.

Some distance away from the wrought-iron gates, he climbed over the high brick wall that surrounded the place, and landed softly in the dense, but well-cultivated shrubbery.

Quickly, he began to move forward, threading his way past the bushes, and leaving a trail of crossed twigs as he went – just in case he ran into trouble.

He stopped by a large rhododendron. The shrubbery ended, giving way to a large expanse of lawn. Barton dropped to the ground in case there was anyone around. A long way away, at the top of the slight rise, he could make out the house. It was an original of the kind that was later copied all over England. The place was a large, stucco and half timbered country house. Even in the fading light, he could make out several stained glass windows. Then, nearby, a sound alerted him and he crawled back into the shrubbery.

He was just in time. There came the thud of heavy boots, and a dark figure carrying a gun under his arm strolled past. There were voices in German. Barton peeked out to see the man who had just strolled past meet another guard. Then, he returned the way he had come.

He waited until the coast was clear and then sprinted

across the lawn towards the house.

Panting, he arrived at a flanking wing. He shrank into the shadow provided, and gradually worked his way round to the front door. It was locked.

It was now completely dark. The special agent went around the perimeter of the house again, trying windows as he went. The patrols were safely in the background. Around the back, french windows gave on to a large verandah. He was in luck. They were open. He waited a moment listening for sounds of activity from inside the house. There were none. He slipped the catch and went inside.

He had closed the windows, and turned in the gloom when he stiffened. Suddenly, the lights were turned on and he was dazzled by the glare.

'Don't move!'

It took several moments for his eyes to become accustomed to the light. At the far end of the room, he made out a group of figures. Muller and Klaus were amongst them.

'It really would be unwise of you to make any kind of move,' the Swiss continued.

Barton held up both arms to show that he had no weapon.

'Good,' said the cultivated voice. 'I like a man who knows when he's beaten.'

'Don't count on it,' the special agent warned.

Muller chuckled as Klaus came across the room and searched Barton for concealed weapons. He didn't find any.

'You again,' Barton commented. 'I should have taken care of you in London, once and for all.'

Klaus murmured something in German, but it was Muller who took up the point:

'Hindsight, Mr Barton, the most futile emotion of them all. All we have to do is to wait for your colleagues to join you.'

'That's what I mean,' Dick Barton allowed himself a slight grin. 'They won't. They're not even here.'

'Donner und Blitzen!' Klaus declared.

'But when I don't get back,' Barton warned Muller, 'they'll come looking for me. On their terms.' He turned to Klaus. 'And that's when you'll get your come-uppance, Fritz, my friend.'

Muller walked across the room towards the special agent.

61

'I think not,' he declared. 'You see this house was only rented for our little charade. Admittedly I had hoped to eliminate all three of you. But since you're the brains, such as they are, of your organisation, such as it is . . . ' he smiled, more than pleased with himself. 'I love the challenge of having to improvise, don't you?' he said as he came closer.

Dick Barton couldn't stand it any longer. He threw himself at Muller, but Klaus and two of the guards were too quick for him. Suddenly, the special agent found himself fighting three men at once. He tried a left hook, but winced as a fist landed in his belly. His knuckles connected with a guard's jaw, but another blow landed on the side of his face. He went down fighting every inch of the way. After a few moments, they held him, panting and bloodied, while Muller advanced slowly.

'I bet you only hit a man when he's down,' Barton declared. 'It goes with making war on women and children.'

'That was a foolish as well as a pointless move,' came the reply. 'Hitherto . . . ' Muller shrugged in his urbane fashion. 'Now you have made the issue personal. I cannot allow that to go unrebuked, if you are to discourage others from following your example.' He turned to Klaus. 'Let us go.'

Dick Barton was then hauled across the room by the two guards. Klaus and Muller followed.

Jock Anderson sat playing patience in George Cameron's sitting room. From time to time he glanced up at a photograph of George and himself that had been taken in Hamburg during the war. It all seemed such a long time ago.

Then the door from the bedroom opened and Snowey White came out yawning. His hair was tousled, and his clothes rumpled.

'How're you feeling?' Jock said.

Snowey grinned. 'A lot better.'

'From where you started that could still be not so good.'

'Funny man,' Snowey replied. He came further into the room and then turned towards the kitchen. 'No word from the guv'nor?' Jock shook his head in reply. 'Should be here by now,' Snowey looked puzzled. 'Oh well. Fancy some grub?' He went into the outer room.

'May as well,' Jock replied. He began turning cards over again.

George and Lucy Cameron stood in the centre of the room while Muller spoke to them. They were surprised at his return. He made no mention of the photographs, but they still lingered in the minds of both father and daughter.

'The situation has changed rather,' Muller announced. He then spoke directly to Lucy. 'I'd appreciate it if you'd collect the rest of the formula.'

'Do your own devil's work,' George Cameron replied.

Muller smiled, he spread his hands in an empty gesture. 'You wanted me to let her go.'

'Yes, but not to ...'

'Oh, what does it matter?' Lucy interrupted.

'I congratulate you on your sense of realism, my dear,' Muller said to Lucy. 'I trust that it will extend to remembering that your father is still here?'

'What if I'm caught?' the girl asked.

'Oh, you won't steal it,' Muller replied slyly. 'We could do that ourselves. The whole idea is not to attract attention by precipitating another brawl,' Muller frowned as he was reminded of the fracas in Tibbs's laboratory. 'You will simply tell White and Anderson that Barton sent you for it.'

'You've got him then?' George Cameron wanted to know if all avenues of escape really were sealed.

'Naturally,' came the reply.

'Suppose he gets a message to them?' Lucy suggested. She had more than a hope that Dick Barton was not yet finished.

'That's hardly likely in the circumstances, my dear,' Muller said as he began to walk towards the door. There was menace in his tone.

Later that same night, the reason behind Muller's prediction became clear. On a lonely beach, Dick Barton looked up at the stars. He didn't have much choice. He was buried up to his neck in the sand. The tide was out, and the special agent realised that for the first, and probably the last time in his life, he would be counting waves as hours.

Above him Klaus beckoned and a figure dressed in an

63

expensive overcoat with an astrakhan collar appeared. It was Muller. Barton glared at him.

'Do you know,' Muller said to the special agent, 'I'm really quite surprised Klaus had it in him. He's usually very physical – as witness the late and unlamented Tibbs.' He gestured towards the sea, 'This is, by any standards, most sophisticated and really admirably thought-out.' He turned to his second in command. 'Very good,' he commented.

Klaus replied in a harsh staccato German. He indicated the sea.

'Yes, yes, I understand,' the Swiss villain said. Then he turned back towards Dick Barton. 'But, so the beauty of it is not lost on you . . . you will be drowned by the incoming tide. As it recedes, it will take your unmarked body with it, to be washed up who knows when or where. Oh, by all means scream, but it is a private beach, and there's an off-shore breeze, as you can no doubt feel. You might be better advised to contemplate the symmetry of Klaus's plan in what little time remains to you. So, Mr Barton, I bid you a fond *adieu*.'

Muller turned on his heel and began to walk away. He beckoned for Klaus to follow.

Dick Barton watched them go. He wasn't sorry to see the last of them. As for his own fate, that was a different matter. According to his own calculations the tide was still going out. As the wind ruffled his hair, and the weight of the sand pressed on his body, he began to feel no fear, but a strong desire to live, and to see justice done.

'Help!' he called out.

The gulls seemed to echo him with their mocking cries.

Has Barton's luck finally run out?
Will Jock and Snowey believe Lucy?
Who put them on to the wrong house?
Can Muller get away with the formula?
Read the next chapter of:
Dick Barton – Special Agent.

Chapter Five

Lucy has been blackmailed into collecting the missing part of the formula. Barton has been lured into a trap. Will Jock and Snowey believe Lucy's story? Barton himself is, literally, in it up to the neck.

Now read on.

It was early morning, the tide was on the turn, and beginning to creep in over the rippled sand. The sun came out from behind a bank of clouds, and the gulls wheeled overhead. The only thing on the beach was a head; it protruded from the sand, from the neck up. The neck was stiff, and the man to whom it belonged grimaced as he realised that his time was running out.

Dick Barton had survived the night, but it now looked as if he would be meeting his watery grave within hours. He called out:

'Hello? Hello-o-o-o-o!'

For a reply there was only the whistle of the chill wind, and the screaming of the gulls, and the incessant lapping sound of the sea.

The special agent composed himself. 'Oh, well,' he said, though there was no one to hear, 'it's been a good innings on the whole.'

Small waves began to break on the beach. The sea was grey and bleak. Prospects looking uninviting.

Snowey White came into Cameron's living room from the bathroom. He'd just had a wash and shave and now feeling completely recovered. Jock was sitting on the settee. Snowey noticed that he was looking at the photograph of himself and George Cameron again. 'Nothing from the governor?' he asked.

'Not a peep.'

'That's it, then. I'm off to have a butchers at that house.'

'He said on no account to leave here until we heard from him,' Jock replied.

Snowey came closer to Jock. 'Yes, but he's been gone all blooming night.'

'He still said . . . '

'Thing about orders is to know when to disobey them, my old china,' Snowey interrupted.

'That's not what they told me in the army.'

Snowey began to walk impatiently around the room. He couldn't stand all this waiting. 'Well, they wouldn't in REME, would they?' he said to Jock. 'In the Commandoes . . . '

'Here we go again,' came the weary reply.

'You learn to use your loaf,' Snowey continued. 'And, let me tell you, the Captain was the first person to elbow orders that didn't fit the facts . . . '

Jock held up his hand for silence. They heard a car approach.

'Speak of the devil.' Snowey started to go out to meet the car.

'Hold it,' Jock said firmly, 'that's no Riley.'

Snowey shrugged. 'They all sound alike to me.'

Jock got up from where he was sitting. 'I'm telling you. That's not Barton's car.'

'I'll nip upstairs and have a dekko,' Snowey replied. When it came to cars, he was sure that Jock knew what he was talking about. He walked across the room.

Outside the home that she had now not seen for several days, Lucy Cameron stepped out of the Jaguar SS-100 that belonged to Klaus. Hesitantly, she looked towards the house

And inside, from a window on the landing, Snowey saw what was happening. 'It's Lucy,' he called out.

From downstairs, Jock Anderson replied, 'Mr Barton must have got her out.'

'I'm not so sure . . . ' Snowey said. He looked out of the window once again. 'Here, Jock, come on up.'

Soon, Jock joined Snowey on the landing.

'You're right,' Snowey said as he pointed out of the window. 'It isn't the guv'nor's car.'

66

'No,' Jock replied as he looked in the direction that Snowey indicated. There was a grim expression on his face. 'That's the car that ran down Tibbs, I'll swear it.' He was sure he was right. It was a 1937 Jaguar SS-100. He'd know it anywhere.

Snowey looked out again, and saw a man lean out of the window of the car. He wore a trilby and a black leather trenchcoat. 'And look who's driving it. The same nasty looking Kraut.'

'I've got a score to settle with him,' Jock answered.

Snowey turned towards his friend. 'So's she. That's the point.'

Jock didn't quite understand what Snowey was getting at.

'Well, look at him,' the ex-sergeant continued, 'rabbiting away. She hasn't said a dickey bird yet.'

Jock looked out again, and this time he saw that Snowey was right. Klaus was gesticulating at Lucy as if he was giving her orders. 'Now what's going on, do you think?' he asked.

Snowey saw Lucy stand on the kerb while the Jaguar drove slowly away. 'He's scarpered.'

'No, hark!' Jock answered. 'The engine's stopped.'

By craning his neck Snowey could just make out the Kraut walking back to a position where he could keep a watch on the house. 'Looks like he's waiting for her.'

Jock then saw Klaus signalling to Lucy, who began to approach the house. 'And neither of them's keen for us to know about it,' he said. His tone was serious.

They turned away from the window together. Both wondered about the implications behind the scene they had just witnessed.

'Better see what she has to say,' Jock commented after a while.

'But watch her,' Snowey warned.

They went down the stairs together.

Meanwhile, Lucy Cameron, aware that Klaus was watching every move that she made, mussed up her hair and clothes, and ran the last few steps to the house. She rang the bell. Jock and Snowey answered the door.

'Lucy!' Snowey seemed glad to see her.

'Quick!' she said.

'Come away in, lass,' Jock added.

67

They bundled her quickly into the house, and, in the background the ex-SS officer called Klaus smiled at the apparent stupidity of his opponents.

Snowey and Jock brought Lucy into the living room of the house. They both sat down but she remained standing in the centre of the room. She looked nervous.

'Mr Barton rescued me,' the girl explained.

'Are you all right?' Jock asked.

'Fine.'

Snowey looked at the girl from where he was sitting. He wondered what was up. 'Where is he?' he said.

'Still at the house,' Lucy bluffed. 'Trying to work things out. He sent me to get the other part of the formula.'

'What for?' Jock Anderson was now very doubtful indeed whether there was any truth behind what his friend's daughter was saying.

'It's a long story.' Lucy looked timidly from Snowey to Jock and then back again.

'I'll bet,' Snowey remarked.

'But he thinks that, if he has it, he may be able to bluff . . . ' Lucy continued her attempt.

'It's a good try, Lucy,' Jock interrupted as he got up and walked across the room to where the girl was standing.

'I'm to go back with it at once,' she said desperately. She was now floundering, unsure that she was convincing them, and fearful for the safety of her father.

When Snowey spoke his tone was flat. 'You might even have got away with it if we hadn't spotted our old pal Klaus,' he remarked.

Jock's question was even more penetrating. 'Where does he fit into all this?'

Suddenly, Lucy darted across the room, grabbed the photograph of Jock and her father in Hamburg, and tried to make a break for it.

'Get her, Jock!' Snowey shouted.

Jock Anderson reached out and stopped Lucy from reaching the door. As he grabbed her, the framed photograph fell to the floor and broke into several pieces.

'Oh,' Lucy said. And, at the back of her mind, she saw another photograph, one of the horrors in Muller's file. Tears began to form in her eyes.

68

'I didna want to hurt you, lass,' Jock said sympathetically as he released his hold on her.

In the meantime, Snowey White had bent down and retrieved the other half of Cameron's formula from amongst the shattered glass and pieces of broken frame. 'Is this what all the fuss is about?' he asked as he held up the formula for Jock to see.

'You don't understand,' the girl declared.

Jock looked thoughtful. It was some time before he spoke. 'All I know is that your father went to a lot of trouble to stop the formula falling into the wrong hands.' He paused to look at Lucy who had now recovered her composure. 'Now you're not going to let him down, are you?'

Once again, the horrors that Muller had threatened forced themselves to her attention. The man was capable of anything. 'It's the only chance of saving his life,' she said to Jock.

'I thought Mr Barton was attending to that,' Snowey put in.

Lucy made an empty gesture with her hands. 'How could he?' she replied. 'He walked into a trap. He's being drowned at this very moment.'

Snowey was suddenly very alert. 'You say the guv'nor's being drowned?' he insisted.

Lucy looked at the ex-sergeant. 'That's what they told me.'

'Then we're still in with a fighting chance,' Jock said to Snowey.

The two friends of the special agent exchanged glances. They were going to have to think something up pretty quickly.

Outside the house, Klaus checked the time while he waited for Lucy to reappear with the formula. He was confident that she would. It should not take long to convince the foolish assistants of Dick Barton. After all, the special agent himself was now facing a very unpleasant end. The ex-SS officer grinned with satisfaction.

Back in the living room of the Cameron house, Snowey had already begun to act. He put down the telephone and grinned at Jock. 'They're on the way,' he said.

'Right.' Jock turned and began to go out of the room.

69

'Oh please!' Lucy cried. 'If it doesn't work . . . '

Jock turned and patted Lucy reassuringly on the arm. Then he continued on his way.

Moving stealthily, Jock Anderson came out of the back door of the Cameron house, sidled along the side wall, and then stopped. He could see Klaus lounging across the road. The Jaguar SS-100 was further away down the street. Using whatever cover there was available, including parked cars and the trees that were planted in a neat line going down the street, Jock managed to reach the car without being seen by the German.

As he ducked down behind the Jaguar, Jock saw Klaus glance up at the house again. Then he got into the unlocked car and quickly made a note of the mileage reading on the speedometer.

He was just in time. A police car, in response to Snowey's phone call, screamed around the corner and into the suburban street.

Jock looked up again in time to see Klaus on the move towards the Jaguar. Muller's assistant had evidently decided to make himself scarce.

When the doorbell rang, Snowey opened the door and found himself confronted by three uniformed policemen. 'An emergency call?' he said in a puzzled fashion. Then he shook his head. He turned and shouted down the hallway. 'You didn't call the lily, did you, Lucy?'

Lucy appeared and joined Snowey on the doorstep. 'No. Why should I?'

'Search me,' Snowey replied innocently. He turned with a blank face towards the three uniformed policemen again. 'If you ask me,' he said, 'it sounds like a practical joke. But now you're here, if you want to, take a look.' He gestured for them to come in.

It was an unnecessary move. The three uniformed officers pushed past Snowey and went into the house.

By this time, Klaus, with a glance backwards over his shoulder at the police on the doorstep of Cameron's house, had reached the car. He opened the door and got quickly into the driver's seat, started the car and drove off at a furious pace.

As he drove, there was a scowl on the German's face. He wondered how such a well-thought-out scheme could have gone wrong, particularly when the brains of the Barton organisation was at this very moment facing an unpleasant demise. In anger, Klaus drove even faster.

Unknown to the former SS officer, he was not alone. Jock Anderson lay stretched out behind the front seats of the car. He kept his head to the floor. But he couldn't resist a slight smile.

Snowey led the police to the front door again. They had naturally found nothing. 'I don't believe in messing with the law myself,' he said, as he let them out, 'but there's some silly so-and-so's about.'

He shut the door again. And, even as she heard the sound of heavy footsteps going down the front path, Lucy Cameron burst out laughing. 'Your injured innocence!' she said to Snowey. 'If I wasn't so desperate, I'd have had to laugh before.'

'That would have blown the gaff,' came the reply.

The seriousness of the situation rapidly reasserted itself. 'How do we know he'll go back to Muller?' Lucy asked suddenly.

'Stands to reason, doesn't it?' Snowey said. He knew what he was talking about. He'd had plenty of experience during the war. 'When things go wrong, your average Kraut's like a chicken with his head cut off. He'll go back to ask what he's to do next.' He looked down with sympathy at the return of a worried expression to Lucy's face. 'Jock'll find your old man and have him out of there before you can say ITMA.'

'I only hope you're right,' the girl replied. She was worried about her father, who was still in the clutches of the over-civilised Swiss villain. She wondered how long it would be before Muller decided to start work on him.

Snowey broke the silence. 'Stand on me, I'm right,' he said. 'So let's get after the guv'nor. And we'd better take the formula with us, just in case.'

Lucy went back into the front room to retrieve the piece of paper that held the secret of her father's fatal discovery,

71

and was the key to his own life and death. She handed it over to Snowey. She trusted Dick Barton and company. She was now back on the right side.

Dick Barton looked around. The tide crept nearer and nearer. There seemed to be no consistent pattern by which he could estimate how much time he had left. The sea came forward in surges, and then seemed to wait. There was no other sign of life on the beach. Now, even the gulls had gone. His lips were dry, and caked with salt from the spray. The tide surged forward again.

The Jaguar SS-100 skidded to a halt. Klaus got out and ran up the drive towards the house. When he was sure that the German had gone, Jock surfaced from the back of the car and noted the speedometer mileage reading once again. Then he got out of the car on the side opposite the house, and began to look around.

It was a large building, and, if the goings on inside it had not been part of a devilish scheme, it could have been called impressive, the mechanic thought. It was brick built, with several storeys and a profusion of bay windows overlooking the drive. Jock contrasted it with his own terraced house, and the rewards of villainy with those of an honest occupation. He wondered whether George Cameron was inside.

Lucy waited by a camouflaged Riley Monaco while Snowey White paid off the taxi that had brought them to the address at which Dick Barton had previously arrived, and where he had been captured by Muller.

'How do we know which way he went?' Lucy asked as the taxi drew away.

'He'll have blazed a trail,' Snowey explained with confidence, as he began to look around. 'See?' he said after a while. 'There!' He pointed to some crossed twigs which lay on the ground at the exact point where Dick Barton had crossed the wall.

Snowey looked dubiously at Lucy for a moment. 'He wouldn't want you to get mixed up in this,' he said.

'Just get on with it,' the girl replied impatiently.

72

Snowey shrugged and then helped her over the wall. Then, he began to climb over himself.

When he landed on the other side of the wall, Snowey, like the special agent before him, was confronted by a dense mass of shrubbery. It took him some time to locate Barton's trail again. When he had found it, he motioned for Lucy to follow behind him.

'Keep your peepers peeled,' Snowey said. 'This is it.'

Jock Anderson was crouched down, ready to make a sprint for the house, when he heard the sound of voices. He couldn't let himself be caught in the open. There was only one thing for it. He opened the boot of the Jaguar, and climbed quickly in. He took the precaution of not closing it down tightly after him, so that, through the crack he could see what was going on.

Muller and Klaus now approached.

'The girl must have betrayed us,' Klaus explained to his superior as they walked.

'Or Barton's people are cleverer than I thought,' the Swiss psychologist remarked.

'That wouldn't be difficult,' came the reply.

Jock located some car rugs in the boot, and buried himself underneath them. From outside, the voices, now muffled slightly, continued.

'Either way,' Muller said. 'Barton may be more useful to us alive than dead.'

'Let's hope that it's not too late,' Klaus's clipped, Germanic tones replied.

'See that it isn't!'

Then, Jock heard Klaus call out, 'Christian! Hans!'

The next thing Jock knew what felt like two shovels were thrown on top of him, and the boot was slammed shut. Then, he heard the sound of the two guards running towards the Jaguar. They got in. The car started and drove off. Jock hoped that they would be in time now that they had had a change of heart about the fate of Dick Barton.

Snowey White ran out of the large country house after following his governor's trail right to a pair of french windows. He ran across the gravel path to where Lucy was standing.

'No wonder they nabbed him,' Snowey said as he came near. 'It's a blooming empty house.'

Lucy Cameron looked worried. She turned to Snowey for guidance. 'Now what?' she asked.

Snowey pointed back towards the way they had come. They both began to run.

The water lapped at the special agent's chin. There was the taste of salt in his mouth, but his throat was dry. Any moment, a wave could swamp him completely. He was preparing to meet his end when he saw a large car screech to a stop on the beach some distance away. He recognised it. It was the Jaguar SS-100 that had run down Tibbs.

Then Klaus and two guards carrying shovels began to run towards him.

'Well,' Dick Barton said to Klaus as he drew near, 'you're the last person I expected to see.'

Klaus scowled at the special agent, and spoke to the guards. 'Dig him out,' he said in German.

Dick Barton understood, and, as the two flunkeys began to shovel sand away from him, he taunted Klaus again. 'Don't tell me you've seen the light?' he said. He even managed a smile at the turn of events.

'The Herr Professor wishes to see you,' Klaus replied with as little expression as possible.

Across the beach, unknown to Dick Barton or Muller's henchmen, Jock Anderson, on the far side of the Jaguar, was busy with the controls. Satisfied with his work, he smiled and started the engine.

The special agent was climbing gratefully out of the hole when he heard the roar from the car. He wasn't the only one; Klaus and company also looked up from their work in time to see the Jaguar weave across the beach, gathering speed as it went.

'What – ?' Klaus was totally perplexed. 'After it!' he shouted to the guards.

And, as they began to run across the beach in obedience to Klaus's command, Dick Barton used the diversion to try and make a break for it.

74

Klaus spotted the move and drew a gun on the special agent. 'Not so fast!' he said.

Barton shrugged and looked across the beach. The Jaguar was still going, and the guards were running after it, firing wild shots as they went.

Then he saw the car begin to climb up a dune. It was too steep. The wheels began to spin in the soft sand. Eventually the engine stalled.

'You see,' Klaus said triumphantly to Barton, 'we're not so easily thwarted.'

Meanwhile, Jock Anderson, as he loped through the dunes towards Barton and Klaus, smiled as he saw the flunkeys flounder through the sand towards the car, and exclaim in amazement when they found no one in it.

Dick Barton saw Jock approach, but said nothing until the mechanic was virtually right behind Klaus. Then, he pointed.

Klaus laughed at the apparent stupidity of the special agent. 'Surely you don't expect me to fall for a trick as old as that?' he said.

Then Jock popped up behind the German. All he said was, 'Peekaboo!'

Klaus spun around, and, as he did so, Dick Barton quickly disarmed him and chopped him down.

'It's good to see you,' Jock remarked.

'I'll thank you later,' Barton replied. He looked across the dunes towards the guards.

Klaus's henchmen were just about recovering from their astonishment that there had been no one in the Jaguar. Now they understood why. When they looked into the car, they saw that the accelerator had been wedged to the floor with a block of wood. They turned and walked back across the beach to report their findings.

When they reached their commander, they found him in the same position as before. Apparently, he was holding a gun on the special agent.

'There was no one in it,' one said in German.

'The accelerator, it was wedged, you see,' the other reported in the same language.

Only when Klaus turned to face them, it wasn't him at all. It was Jock Anderson with Klaus's hat, coat and gun. Their commander's unconscious body lay stretched out on the beach. One of them made a dive for Jock.

The Scotsman parried the blow. Dick Barton came to his assistance. The second guard joined in, but he didn't last long. The special agent felled him with an uppercut. The struggle was soon over. Dick Barton relished his chance of getting some of his own back at last. Soon, two more unconscious bodies joined Klaus on the sand.

Jock Anderson glanced from the defeated enemy to the hole from which Dick Barton had just been released. A slow smile spread over his face. 'What do you say?' he asked the special agent.

Barton grinned in reply. 'It seems only just.'

And so they set to work.

About ten minutes later, Jock and Barton walked over to the Jaguar. Jock noted the mileage reading again. He looked at Barton, and they laughed together. Just before Jock started the car, the ex-captain of commandos turned to look at their handiwork.

Across the beach, Klaus and his assistants were buried up to their necks in sand. The tide was lapping at them.

Barton nodded at Jock, and they drove off.

Gustave Muller, Professor of Psychology, and the perpetrator of ruthless deeds, came out of his country house headquarters and checked the time. A worried frown crossed his face. He turned, and with a click of his fingers, summoned the nearest lackey. He spoke to him in German:

'Take three men and find out what's happened to Klaus,' he ordered. He didn't mention Dick Barton. But, if possible, he did want the special agent alive.

The man he had talked to summoned three others. They piled into a waiting estate car and drove off.

Snowey White had decided that the best course of action was to return to Merton's and discuss the situation with the General. He was telling Lucy about him as they stood in the outer laboratory of what had once been Tibbs's workplace.

'You haven't met General Wilson, have you?'

'No.'

Snowey smiled to himself. 'You've got a treat in store, I'm telling you.'

Almost as soon as Snowey had finished speaking, the General himself, accompanied by his personal assistant, bustled in. 'Now then,' he said. 'Which one of you's Lucy?'

'The other one, sir,' came Snowey's reply.

'Ah, yes,' the General said. He turned to Lucy. 'Bad business, my dear. Can't tell you how sorry I am.'

Lucy cut through the General's blustering. 'It need never have happened if you'd answered Dad's note.'

A look of surprise came over Wilson. 'Note? What note's that?'

'When we realised what he'd discovered,' Lucy explained patiently. 'He wrote to tell you about it.' She paused for effect. 'You never even answered.'

The General glanced at his personal assistant. 'We never heard from him, did we Ashe?'

The pale-faced young man answered his superior in bland tones. 'Not to my knowledge, General.'

Lucy was now perplexed; she knew that her father had definitely written. 'But he told me . . . ' she began again.

Enlightenment dawned on the General's face. 'You know what happened?' he interrupted. 'Those bounders intercepted it.'

'Very possibly,' Ashe conceded.

Snowey shifted restlessly. It took them such a long time to see the obvious.

'Typical Swiss trick,' the General said as he started one of his customary speeches. 'Like harbouring Lenin. Not a lot of people know that. There might never have been a Russian revolution without the Swiss. Think of that. Mind you, Joe Stalin's not a bad sort.' He must have sensed Snowey's impatience, because he looked at him and said, 'I don't like to think of Barton being drowned, though.'

Neither did Snowey. Nor Lucy.

As Snowey was pondering the next step, and wishing that General Wilson would hurry things up, Muller's four henchmen were busy on the same deserted beach where Barton had been buried up to his neck in the sand. They were

77

digging Klaus and their comrades out of the same hole. They weren't pleased about it.

When Dick Barton and Jock returned to the laboratory, they were greeted with great relief by Snowey, Lucy and Wilson. The special agent had immediately explained what they had done with Muller's men. There was laughter all round.

'I felt a bit bad about it afterwards,' Barton explained on a more thoughtful note.

'Nonsense,' the General replied. 'Serve the blighters right.'

Snowey, now that the guv'nor was back, was trying to sort out what exactly had happened. 'What I want to know,' he remarked, 'is why that estate agent put me on to the wrong house.'

'We don't know that he did,' Ashe put in quickly.

'How do you work that out?' the special agent wanted to know.

Ashe breathed deeply. 'Well, if it was to be a trap, surely they'd have to have taken that house as well as the one they're really using as a base.' He turned to Snowey. 'You just picked the wrong one.'

'Bad habit of yours that, White,' Wilson chimed in. 'Blaming other people all the time. *Qui s'excuse a mal y pense.*'

Snowey was furious. He knew that Ashe was crooked, but, as yet, he couldn't prove it. He said nothing.

Lucy didn't think it was profitable to waste time blaming others either. And she trusted Snowey far more than the General. 'They've still got Dad,' she reminded the Chairman of Merton Fertilizers.

'Yes,' Dick Barton said confidently. 'But we know where he's being kept now.'

'How?'

'I took the mileage to it from your place,' Jock explained to the girl. 'And then from it to the beach. With distances from two fixed points we can work it out.'

'Well done that man,' Wilson commented.

'And we've got the business end of the formula,' Barton announced.

Ashe showed a keen interest as soon as the formula was

.mentioned. 'Don't you think perhaps it might be better kept in the safe?' he asked solicitously.

'Good thinking,' Wilson commended his assistant. He watched as Dick Barton handed over the vitally important document. 'You've got to admit he has his moments,' he added.

And so Ashe took the formula, and began to walk out of the room. Everyone believed that he was going to place it in the safe. But, if they could have seen the smile on his face at that moment, they might have thought differently.

'Now where are those maps?' Dick Barton asked.

Muller was furious. He stood in the hall of his headquarters and screamed abuse at the bedraggled Klaus who stood penitently before him. 'You bungling idiot! You devise an ingenious punishment and then let the fools trap you in it while they escape.'

His superior spoke in German. Klaus bowed his head as he took the rebuke he deserved. But he was far from pleased at being placed in such an unpleasant situation.

Then the telephone rang. Muller picked it up immediately. 'Ja?' He changed to English. 'Who's this?' There was a pause. 'Perfect. Quite perfect.' His expression changed to a smile and then he broke out into uproarious laughter.

Klaus began to look happier as Muller issued fresh instructions.

What has Muller got to be so pleased about?
Can Ashe be trusted with the formula?
Are things less straightforward than they seem?
Read the next chapter of:
Dick Barton – Special Agent.

Chapter Six

Dick Barton has been released from his watery grave, and with Jock's help is trying to locate the headquarters of the Swiss villain Gustave Muller. But, George Cameron's formula has been given to Ashe for safekeeping. The scientist himself is still prisoner.

Now read on.

Ashe came out into the yard surrounding the fertilizer factory. He walked over to the Jaguar SS-100 that was still parked there. The keys were in the ignition. He was relieved. He glanced towards the laboratory block, and, after making sure that no one had seen him, he got into the car and drove off.

Dick Barton, Snowey and Jock were now poring over the maps which were spread out on a laboratory bench. Thanks to Jock's clever detective work, they had a clear idea where to look.

'There's the beach,' the special agent said as he pointed with his finger.

'Right,' Jock replied. 'We know their base is two and three-tenths of a mile from that.' Using the pencil and compasses that he was holding, he began to mark off the circumference of a circle inland from the location Barton had shown. That completed, he spoke again; 'And it's four and seven-tenths of a mile from Cameron's house.' He began to draw another circle.

'Bingo!' Snowey White shouted suddenly. He'd just seen the circles intersect at the location of a large house.

'Inkerman Place,' Dick Barton added.

'It's about the right size,' Jock added.

'And the right distance,' continued the special agent.

'Oh, blimey O'Reilly!' Snowey called out suddenly. 'Look out!'

General Wilson, full of his own importance as usual, blundered into the room. 'Look here, Barton . . . ' and then, seeing the others were now looking pleased with themselves, he changed his tone. 'Got it all sorted out?'

'We're working on it,' the special agent replied coldly.

'Jolly good,' Wilson came over to the bench and started to look at the maps and the drawing equipment. 'Trigonometry, is it?' he asked in a puzzled fashion.

'Geometry,' Jock said. He wasn't encouraging either.

'You don't say?' the General burbled on. 'Flunked both at Wellington myself. Would have been ploughed for Sandhurst if it hadn't been for this crammer.' His face lit up at the memory. 'Wonderful chap. I remember he explained it all with a hat and a stick and a handkerchief. Forgotten it now, of course. Still, that's the way of it.' An absent-minded expression took hold of him. 'Where was I? Ah, yes.' He looked in the direction of the special agent. 'Look here, Barton, I'm more than willing to give you all the help you need but sending off my personal assistant to run your errands without so much as a by your leave . . . Don't you think that's a bit thick?'

'Ashe?' Snowey cut in.

Barton looked at the General with distaste. He had never liked interfering busybodies. Particularly when they had more rank than sense. 'I don't know what you're talking about,' he declared.

'He's just driven off in the dashed car you took from those blighters,' Wilson explained in a more reasonable tone.

'Stop him, Jock,' Barton ordered.

'Oh, it's too late for that,' the General shook his head. 'Far too late.'

'Forget it.' Barton cancelled his command.

' 'sides, I don't want to make a mountain out of Mahomet,' Wilson continued.

Snowey felt justified at last. 'I told you he was as bent as a hairpin, didn't I?'

Wilson looked shamefaced. 'I'm well aware that you've

6   81

never cared for the fellow, White,' he said. 'If you must know I'm not over-enamoured of him myself. He's a cold fish. And I think he could have got himself accepted for National Service if he'd put his mind to it,' he continued irrelevantly. 'Hang it all, flat feet never stopped Napoleon, did they? Or do I mean Alexander the Great?' Then he realised that no one was really listening to his rambling. 'That's not the point,' he corrected himself.

'The point is I never asked him to do anything for us,' Barton commented succinctly.

'Well I'm blessed!' said Wilson in amazement. 'What do you think it means?'

Barton was pleased that Snowey had been vindicated. 'It could mean that he's working for the other side,' he replied slowly.

'Give him his due,' Jock Anderson urged. 'He may have been leaned on.'

'Or half inched, come to that,' Snowey added.

'Either way we'd better make sure the formula's safe,' the special agent concluded.

Wilson nodded sagely in agreement. 'By jove, yes.' Then, the realisation struck him. 'No, damn. We can't.'

'Why not?' Jock wanted to know.

The General avoided looking the mechanic in the eyes. 'Ashe changed the combination last night. He's the only person who knows it.'

'I don't believe it!' Snowey exclaimed.

Wilson felt compelled to justify his own administration. He got his proverbs mixed up again. 'Security, d'you see?' he tried to explain. 'Too many cooks spill the lock.'

Dick Barton wanted the plain facts – with all the elaborations, frills and mixed metaphors left out. 'Ashe's idea?' he asked.

'I believe it was, now you come to mention it,' Wilson admitted.

Snowey raised his eyes. 'God help us all.'

'Amen to that,' seconded the General.

But the special agent was more practical. It was vitally important that they discover whether the formula was still in the safe. 'Better get a locksmith,' he announced.

Jock Anderson made a suggestion: 'Let me take a look at it first,' he said.

Barton agreed with a nod.

Ashe stood by the Jaguar in the drive of the country house. Klaus was with him. Then the front door opened and Muller strode out towards them.

'Do you have it?'

Ashe reached into his inside pocket and produced the document that could, in the wrong hands, threaten the safety of the world. He handed it to Muller. 'Here,' he said.

There was silence while the Swiss eagerly scanned the information. When he looked up he was smiling. 'An excellent piece of work, Ashe. Naturally your commission will be increased.'

'Thank you.'

'I believe in incentives,' Muller commented. 'Did anyone see you leave?'

'I don't think so.'

'Better still,' Muller said after a moment's thought. 'Klaus will drive you home. You can be back before you're missed.'

Fear showed in the eyes of the personal assistant. He had taken a big chance. He felt that he had done enough. 'No,' he said simply.

Muller adopted a wheedling tone; 'Just for a few hours. I don't want their suspicions aroused until we've had a chance to test this,' he indicated the formula. 'A few hours is all I ask.'

Ashe now began to panic at the thought of returning. 'As far as I'm concerned they're already suspicious,' he explained. 'There was that business with the house. The girl's asking questions about that letter her father wrote. Now, this.'

'Be reasonable . . . ' Muller began.

Ashe interrupted him. 'I'm not going back, and that's flat.'

Klaus spoke menacingly to Muller in German. 'Let me deal with him,' he said.

'No, no,' Muller replied. He turned to the traitor again. 'Klaus thinks I should remonstrate with you,' he said. Then, in German, he spoke to Klaus. 'When the time comes to

83

make our getaway we may need something to throw to the wolves.'

Ashe heard the words, though he didn't understand the language. The implication was clear. And, when Klaus burst out laughing, he began to feel even more afraid. He had a feeling that, if necessary, they would be ruthless enough to sacrifice him. He was right.

Muller then behaved in a more diplomatic fashion. 'Myself,' he said, 'I'm philosophical. Since you feel so strongly . . . ' he waved his hands. 'You'll take good care of him, Klaus, won't you?'

The ex-SS officer smiled. 'A pleasure, Herr Professor.'

In the office of Merton Fertilizers, Jock Anderson was fiddling with the combination lock on the safe. He was having some difficulty in judging the sound of the tumblers as the room was packed, and everybody was tending to talk at once. Snowey and Lucy were discussing the defection of Ashe, while Barton and General Wilson were having their own conversation.

'He took that car, didn't he?' Snowey said.

Lucy nodded at him across the room. 'Who else could have intercepted that letter Daddy wrote?'

Snowey was glad that people were agreeing with him for once; it made a change from being treated like a blooming feed in a music hall. 'Who was it made sure we got the particulars of the wrong house?'

Now General Wilson joined in. 'I don't like to damn a man behind his back, but you've got to admit the evidence mounts up.'

'And it's all circumstantial,' Dick Barton reminded him. 'It's not so much that we need to know as that we need to know what the enemy knows.'

Wilson was very impressed. 'Say that again? No. Don't. Got it. You know, Barton, that's jolly good.'

'It's the basis of all intelligence work,' the special agent explained. He knew what he was talking about.

Wilson's expression changed from admiration to one of amazement. 'Is it? Is it really? Wish I'd known that. Could have shortened the war.' Then, when he saw the look that the special agent gave him he added, 'In my command at any rate.'

Jock Anderson turned around in exasperation. He'd been trying to listen for the tumblers falling into place as he turned the dial on the combination lock. 'Well,' he said, 'if you'd all shut up and let me listen I might get somewhere now.' Then, he looked across the room to where the General was standing. 'Sorry, sir.'

Wilson was quite nonchalant about the outburst. 'Not a bit of it,' he replied. 'You're the expert.'

In the silence that followed, Jock set to work again.

Muller, with an expectant expression across his well-fed face, came out of his country house headquarters and began to walk around the back of the house towards the gardens. He was accompanied by Klaus and Ashe. The last member of the party did not look so content; he was worried about his future now that the formula had been delivered, as well he might be.

The group stopped near the entrance to a large hothouse that was filled with a colourful display of azaleas, lilies, and honey coloured orchids. Near the doorway, George Cameron was getting into a protective suit complete with visor.

'When you're ready,' Muller said.

Cameron pulled on the headpiece, and then produced a tiny phial of colourless liquid from a container that had been standing nearby. He went into the greenhouse.

'If it works, will you really let him go?' Ashe asked the Swiss villain, as inside, the scientist carefully unstoppered the phial and began to sprinkle the contents around the greenhouse.

'Why not?' Muller looked surprised at Ashe's question.

'Well, the competition . . . '

Muller looked at the traitor with some distaste. 'Long term greed, my dear Ashe,' he said haughtily, 'is the true sign of the amateur. By the time the competition is organised there may be an antidote. There will certainly be international controls. Long before then I shall have realised the benefits of being first in the field. And moved on.'

'To what?' Ashe asked. He was concerned about the implications of what he was already involved in. He could not conceive of progressing to a greater villainy.

'Don't be crass,' Muller replied. 'One can't anticipate. If one is in the right place, at the right time, opportunities present themselves. One has to be able to recognise them, that's all.'

George Cameron then came out of the greenhouse, and began to remove his protective clothing. Muller glanced at the scientist, and then into the greenhouse behind him. There was no change in the condition of the plants. He spoke to Cameron:

'I have to tell you that I'm not overly impressed so far.'

The scientist seemed unperturbed. He carried on taking off the protective clothing. 'It'll work in just a while,' he said quietly.

Muller turned in the direction of the house. His attitude was one of doubt. 'When it does,' he said, 'it will be my pleasure to reunite you with your daughter.' He issued instructions to Klaus before walking away. 'Call me when something happens.'

Jock Anderson listened as the tumblers on the combination lock clicked slowly into place. Everything felt right. He turned the handle slightly and the safe door swung open.

'Well,' Snowey White commented. 'I always knew you were a load of of tea leaves in REME.'

Jock grinned back. 'All done with mirrors,' he said.

Dick Barton took a step forward and checked the contents of the safe. He rifled quickly through several documents, but did not find the formula. 'It's not there,' he said to the others. 'That settles it. We'd better get cracking and pull George out of there before they make him tie the two parts of the formula together.'

General Wilson puffed out his chest and now joined the special agent. 'If you'll have me, Barton,' he volunteered. 'I'd be happy to serve under you.'

'Happy to have you sir,' Dick Barton confirmed.

The General beamed with pleasure.

'Well, I'm coming, whether you like it or not,' Lucy Anderson announced from the other side of the room.

A frown crossed Dick Barton's face. 'There's no place for a woman in this show, Lucy.' His tone was gentle.

'Then you'll have to make one, won't you?'

The special agent could see that the girl was determined. But he had no time to stop and argue with her now. He began to walk towards the door. 'Talk some sense into her, Jock,' he ordered.

Snowey and Wilson joined him, and they went out of the office together.

'It could turn into a bit of a rough house,' Jock tried to explain to Lucy.

'He's my father,' she said. She thought it was ludicrous that she should be left out just because she was a woman. She could look after herself.

'I've no time to be reasonable, either,' Jock remarked as he quickly followed the others. He closed the office door after him, and, with Lucy still inside, turned the key in the lock.

The girl quickly realised what had happened. She took hold of the door handle and gave it a twist. It was no good. 'Let me out!' she screamed. Then, when there was no reply, she crossed over to the window and looked out into the yard. She was in time to see Jock, Snowey and Barton pile hurriedly into the Riley Monaco. Then, the car drove off.

Lucy looked around the room in a fury. Then, on the floor near the safe, she saw that Jock Anderson, in his hurry to get away, had forgotten his tools. There was a large crowbar amongst them. She picked it up, and approached the door with a determined gleam in her eye. She had no intention of being left out. Not when her own father's life was at stake. She began to work on the lock.

Gustave Muller ran towards the greenhouse at a speed which, had he not heard the extraordinary news, he would have considered to be undignified. The gravel crunched under the soles of his hand-made shoes. And then, suddenly, he stopped.

He could scarcely believe it. The results exceeded his wildest ambitions. For what had been a colourful display of plants only ten minutes previously had turned into an arid and parched display of death. Every shrub, flower and plant was burnt out and withered. There was no sign of a living green shoot. Even the soil had turned to a drifting dust.

Muller turned away from the greenhouse to where George Cameron, Ashe and Klaus were standing.

'Just, suddenly – while we were watching . . . ' the traitor snapped his fingers to indicate the suddenness by which desolation had struck.

Even Klaus was visibly shaken. 'Um Gottes willen,' he murmured.

Muller smiled a slow smile. A fortune was within his grasp. And soon he would be famous, even infamous. 'You have exceeded my fondest hopes,' he said to George Cameron.

The scientist did not look up. He felt that he had violated every code of his profession. 'I'm ashamed of myself,' his voice was almost a whisper. He could not look at the scene of the destruction that he had perpetrated.

Then, the moment was broken. A guard shouted something in German from the house.

'What was that?' Ashe asked.

Muller shrugged dismissively. 'It seems that the dogged Barton and his merry men are about to launch another forlorn hope.'

Dick Barton, accompanied by Snowey, Jock and Wilson, lay under cover in a dense mass of rhododendrons at the front of Muller's headquarters. They were watching the front of the house, but, as yet, had seen nothing very spectacular. They had no notion of the lethal consequences of the experiment that had just been carried out a few hundred yards from where they lay hidden.

'Lying a bit doggo, aren't they?' Snowey said after a while.

'I haven't seen a soul yet,' Jock added.

'Probably choosing their ground,' the special agent announced.

Wilson had been mentally planning an attack. But he had a problem. 'If we had enough men . . . ' he began ponderously.

'Well, we don't,' the man who was really in charge of the situation interrupted. Barton made a decision. 'Right. We'll smoke them out. Remember that stunt we pulled off outside Castelmonte?' he said to Snowey.

'Not half.' The ex-sergeant grinned. They'd had some good times back then.

'Work your way round the back and repeat it,' Barton said tersely. 'We'll seal off this exit. Good luck.'

And so Snowey White, using whatever cover was available, raced off towards the back of the house.

The others waited in silence.

George Cameron stood sandwiched between two guards. The greenhouse was in the background. Muller was nearby. The guards held the scientist firmly. One had rolled up the sleeve of his shirt to expose his bare forearm. The other was preparing an injection, and, from time to time, glanced threateningly at his captive.

'I might have known you'd not keep your word,' Cameron said to the Swiss Villain.

'You malign me,' Muller replied. 'I simply don't want you revealing anything you might have gleaned of our plans until I've had a chance to put them into effect.'

The scientist eyed the syringe, which was now almost ready. 'Well, killing me's a sure way to do that,' he said in a resigned tone.

Muller gestured that Cameron was being unreasonable. 'Please,' he said. 'Don't be melodramatic.'

The scientist looked away as he felt the prick of the needle.

Snowey White was now surrounded by undergrowth at the back of the house. He had a piece of rope with him which he attached to the shrubbery some distance away. He made no effort to move quietly. He wanted a diversion. He jumped up and down so that he could be seen, and pretended to wave someone forward. Then he ducked down again and pulled on the rope so that the shrubbery moved. He raced across to the other side, and jumped up again. He hurled a stone which crashed through the undergrowth. He blew on a whistle. And he clouted a tree with a stick.

Then, he began a frantic series of dashes.

'Now,' he shouted.

He raced through the bushes again.

'Down.'

And again.

'Cover me, Jock.'

He dashed once more.

'Get back.'

Altogether, he succeeded in making an unholy rumpus.

Snowey's 'attack' could be heard even from the front of the house where Dick Barton and company were still lying low. From their position, it sounded as if an army was moving in on Muller and his henchmen.

'Well, now you know,' the special agent said to Wilson.

'Good old Snowey,' Jock added.

There was a look of admiration on the General's face. 'Amazing,' he said.

But, from a vantage point on a knoll outside the house, Gustave Muller was able to see what was going on. He saw Snowey in the bushes at the back, and was also able to spot the ambush that Dick Barton had laid for him at the front.

He put down his binoculars for a moment, and turned to Klaus who was by his side. Ashe stood some distance away. Muller indicated to Klaus that they would get out the back way. The German nodded, and with signs, suggested using Ashe as a decoy. Muller nodded in agreement.

'What's going on?' Ashe said.

'They're sending their main force round the back,' Muller lied. 'We'll create a diversion. When it's working, I'll signal to you. Take the Jaguar and get out fast.' He pointed towards the spot where Barton and company lay hidden. He smiled. 'Didn't I say I'd look after you?'

'Thank you very much,' the unsuspecting traitor replied. He really was very grateful.

Snowey paused from his diversionary activities to mop his brow with a handkerchief, and it was then, through the undergrowth, that he saw something which disturbed him greatly.

He could see the collection of vehicles in the back of the house. Muller Klaus and two guards got into a car and a truck parked in the yard. But Ashe got into the Jaguar SS-100 and turned it to head towards the front gate.

Snowey realised what had happened. He didn't stop to

think. He began to run to try and warn Dick Barton in time.

It was the special agent himself who spotted Snowey in the distance. He appeared to be signalling frantically.

Then, Jock Anderson, who was lying by Barton's side, also saw the activity. 'What the devil's Snowey playing at?'

But the signals became so clear that even General Wilson had little trouble in deciphering them. 'That's "Close on me", he's signalling, isn't it?' he muttered.

'Come on,' Barton said. He was already on his feet.

And so they all broke cover and began to run towards the house.

Muller stood in the yard near the Jaguar. He signalled to Ashe, and the pale-faced young traitor began to drive the Jaguar towards the front of the house.

The Swiss professor of villainy nodded in satisfaction as he saw the car pick up speed. 'Idiot!' he said. Then he walked over to join Klaus and the guards.

Their convoy then proceeded in a leisurely manner in the opposite direction.

Dick Barton and company were confronted by two guards as they came up the drive towards the front of the house. They were wondering how to tackle the situation when a Jaguar SS-100 roared around the corner and made them scatter.

It was at that moment that Lucy Cameron, having escaped from the office and made her own way to the spot where her father was held captive, appeared lower down the drive, out of sight of the car.

'Wait for me,' she shouted as she ran after them.

'Dear heaven, it's Lucy,' Jock shouted.

'Get off the road!' Barton yelled at the girl.

'She can't see him coming,' Wilson warned.

The car was now closing on them fast. Dick Barton made a split-second decision and jumped into the path of the approaching vehicle.

From their different positions, Jock, Wilson, and Lucy watched in amazement.

And, inside the car, the traitor called Ashe clenched his

teeth. He was determined to run the special agent down.

Dick Barton stood his ground.

Then, at the last moment, Ashe lost his nerve. He jammed hard on the brakes bringing the car to a halt inches from the man he lacked the ruthlessness to kill.

'By God, Barton,' said the General. 'That's the bravest thing I ever saw.'

Lucy now approached. 'What did you do that for?' she asked innocently.

'To save your silly little life,' came the reply.

Lucy looked shamefaced. Dick Barton took a deep breath. Ashe was looking even paler than previously. The General took him into custody. They all moved towards the house.

But, in a sense, they were already too late. Muller's convoy was already trundling unhurriedly past the furious Snowey White, and the Swiss villain himself was waving regally.

A few minutes later, Dick Barton, Jock and Snowey entered the devastated greenhouse. The special agent bent down over the unconscious body of George Cameron. Lucy joined him.

'Is he all right?' the girl asked.

Dick Barton felt the scientist's pulse, and then looked at his pupils. 'Doped to the eyeballs, but yes, I think so.'

Jock surveyed the arid destruction of plant life that surrounded them. 'Well, they've got the formula right,' he said. His voice was grim.

'And it works,' Snowey added.

Lucy was more hopeful. 'They haven't got the third part,' she said. And then, when Dick Barton looked questioningly at her, 'Dad told me. There's a third part.'

Snowey looked at the remains of what had once been a red azalea. He would never have known. 'Looks like he's given it to them.'

'Never,' Lucy insisted. 'Though he might have used it himself.'

'To bid for time, you mean?' Jock said. 'Hoping we'd show up?'

Lucy was about to nod in reply when she heard the sound of a car driving away very fast. She wondered what it was.

Dick Barton looked down at the unconscious body of

George Cameron. 'It'll be a while before he's able to tell us,' he remarked.

Jock Anderson had also heard the car. And, with his mechanic's intuition, had recognised it. 'There goes the Jag,' he said.

'Blooming Ashe!' Snowey White was not pleased.

When they reached the front of the house, a crestfallen General Wilson greeted them. 'Look here Barton,' he burbled, 'I feel fairly foolish. The fact of the matter is the rotter said he wanted to relieve himself. Naturally I turned my back. Next thing I knew . . .'

'So much for honour among thieves,' the special agent replied as the General tailed off.

Jock Anderson then held up what appeared to be a piece of machinery. 'He'll not get far without this,' he said.

Snowey looked perplexed. 'What is it?'

Jock smiled. 'The brake linkage,' he said.

'Good on you, Jock,' Dick Barton congratulated the mechanic. He was already heading for his Riley Monaco. 'Let's get after him.' 'Look after Lucy,' he said to Wilson as Snowey and Jock hurried with him towards the car.

What will Muller do next?
Has George Cameron given in or fooled him?
How far can Ashe get in a car with no brakes?
Read the next chapter of:
Dick Barton – Special Agent.

Chapter Seven

Ashe has stolen George Cameron's formula and delivered it to the Swiss villain Muller. Under pressure, the scientist performed a small trial which demonstrated its deadliness. Dick Barton and company arrived at Muller's headquarters – but the villain escaped. After saving Lucy's life, Barton set out after Ashe who was driving a car with no brakes.

Now read on.

The Jaguar SS-100 was travelling fast along the narrow country road. Ashe, now making his second escape attempt, was more determined than ever to succeed. When he turned quickly around to check on his pursuers, he saw the sleek black shape of Dick Barton's Riley Monaco some distance away. But it was gaining.

The special agent himself was behind the wheel of his car. Thanks to Jock's careful maintenance, the car responded to the slightest touch of the accelerator. Dick Barton touched it now.

And, in his car, Ashe responded with more speed. He smiled confidently as the rev. counter flickered upward.

Jock, who was sitting in the passenger seat, smiled grimly at Barton. From behind, Snowey leant over the seat and urged him on.

Then the Jaguar streaked away from them and went into a steep bend.

Inside the Riley Monaco, Jock Anderson shook his head knowingly.

Ashe knew that he had taken a chance by approaching the bend so fast. He swung wide on to the opposite side of the road, and pushed down the brake pedal. Nothing happened.

And now he was nearly on the bend. The situation was looking desperate. Beads of sweat stood out on his forehead. He stamped hard on the brake pedal. There was still no response.

He glanced down and saw that the brake pedal was hanging loose. There was nothing he could do about it. There was a terrible moment when he realised that he was going to crash. And then there was a blur as the hedge on the side of the road suddenly loomed up in front of him. His grip tightened on the steering wheel.

Jock Anderson closed his eyes as he heard the squeal of tyres and the sound of rending metal. Dick Barton slowed the Riley.

'Let's hope the perisher hasn't been and gone and killed his silly self,' Snowey White said from the back of the car.

They all got out to inspect the damage. It wasn't a pretty sight. The Jaguar was a complete write-off. It had ploughed up the bank at the side of the road and smashed into a tree. Ashe hung limply over the steering wheel. Snowey and Jock went in and dragged him out. He didn't resist.

Some time later, in the laboratory of Merton's, General Wilson looked up as the door opened and Dick Barton came in. He was followed by Snowey and Jock. They frog-marched Ashe between them. His face was white and he was shaking. Neither Jock nor Snowey seemed too concerned.

'Don't let me get too near him,' Wilson said angrily. 'I can't answer for what might happen.'

'I ought to see a doctor,' the traitor complained.

Jock Anderson forced the former personal assistant on to a stool. 'Just sit down and shut up,' he ordered.

'He's hardly scratched,' Barton told the General.

'Shock. Concussion,' Ashe moaned.

Jock Anderson stood menacingly over him. 'Shouldn't drive a car without brakes if you can't take a joke,' he said.

Snowey stood on the other side of the recaptured prisoner. 'You're lucky to be blooming alive, you twerp!' He wasn't friendly.

Wilson now walked over. 'By the time I've finished with you that may be in doubt,' he declared. 'Bite the hand that rocks the cradle, would you?' Words almost failed him. He went red in the face. 'You, you worm in the grass.'

Dick Barton's words were more to the point. 'Where's Muller gone?' he asked the shaking prisoner. Then he turned to Wilson. 'Sorry, sir.'

But this was one occasion when the General didn't mind being interrupted. 'No, quite right,' he replied. 'First things first. I've got all the time in the world to deal with him. Fearful thought.'

Snowey glanced disgustedly at Ashe. The man was now snivelling, and yet only a few hours ago if it hadn't been for the guv'nor he would probably have run Lucy Cameron down. 'Want me to work on him, sir?' he asked Barton.

'You'd love that, wouldn't you?' Jock commented.

'Not half,' said Snowey. He closed threateningly on Ashe. 'You and me've got some scores to settle, haven't we? Calling me a liar and giving me the worst hangover I've ever had in my life.'

Ashe shook even more. He was now a pitiable sight.

'The game's up, Ashe,' Barton said flatly.

'Now, are you going to come clean?' Snowey continued. 'Or am I going to have to give you a knuckle sandwich?'

'A knuckle sandwich?' Wilson repeated. He looked perplexed. Then, when Dick Barton showed him a clenched fist, he understood. 'A revolting expression for a barbaric thought.'

Snowey held a fist in front of Ashe's face. 'You've got while I count to three to think about it,' he said.

The General was not so sure about this method of treatment. 'I say, steady on now,' he blustered.

Snowey started counting. 'One.'

'I mean to say,' Wilson continued. 'I don't hold any brief for the fellow, goodness knows, but four against one –'

'Two.'

Ashe quailed before Snowey's threat. 'I'll tell you anything you want to know,' he said suddenly.

Snowey lowered his fist. 'Pity.'

'Where's Muller?' Barton asked.

Ashe looked around desperately. 'I don't know!' Real fear showed in his eyes as Snowey threatened him again. 'I swear it.'

'All right, Snowey,' the special agent said. His second in command lowered his fist again. 'Do you know what his plans are?' he asked the traitor in a gentler tone.

'Not really.'

'You were bluffing, weren't you?' Wilson asked Snowey.

'I wouldn't bet on it,' the ex-sergeant said cheerfully.

Ashe looked at Barton again. He was scared of that man White. He thought he really might get nasty. 'He means to make money out of it, I'm sure,' he said.

'Because you were going to get a cut?'

'Well, yes,' Ashe confessed reluctantly.

'How did you come across him anyway?'

'He contacted me when I got this job,' came the reply.

'And?'

The traitor looked down at the floor. 'Told me there was money to be made from selling industrial secrets.'

'You didn't think to tell me?' Wilson said. 'Let alone send him away with a flea in his ear?'

Ashe looked around the room for sympathy. He didn't find much. The General looked the most likely, so he directed his remarks to him. 'Well, no.' Then he hesitated. 'It was all very theoretical. There was nothing to report. I wasn't even sure what he was saying. I've no idea whether he meant it.'

Wilson was affected by this plea. After all, Ashe had been working for him. It wasn't as if they were strangers. 'Yes, I can see that,' he mumbled. Then he spoke to Barton. 'I always have been able to see the other fellow's point of view. Seldom helps.' He looked thoughtful. 'In fact, I'd say it was the bane of my life.'

Ashe now tried to press home his advantage with Wilson. 'When Cameron sent that letter to you I thought I'd try it out,' he said. 'As a test.' The General seemed to be swallowing his explanation. 'For . . . well, fun, more or less.' He shook his head in despair. 'Only the whole thing got out of hand.'

It was not that Dick Barton lacked a certain amount of sympathy, but there were vital facts that they were still not sure of. 'How many parts were there to the formula?' he demanded.

'Two.'

'Is that all?' Jock cut in.

'Yes.'

'Are you sure?'

'Quite,' Ashe confirmed.

'And George Cameron showed that it worked,' Barton mused.

'Yes,' Ashe replied eagerly. He now wanted to help as much as he could. 'That's the first time I realised – I mean really realised – just how serious the whole thing was. Only then Muller double-crossed me and . . . '

Dick Barton was no longer listening. It was not explanations about the past that he was interested in, but rather what might still happen in the future. The threat had by no means evaporated. In fact, in some ways, it was even more severe than ever. 'We'd better get over to the hospital and see if George has come round,' he said to Jock. 'You stay here,' he ordered Snowey, 'and do whatever the General wants done with Ashe.'

Then the special agent joined Jock who was already waiting at the door. They went out together.

Snowey white looked at Ashe, then at General Wilson, then back to the prisoner again. He rubbed his hands. 'What's it to be, sir?' he said. 'Boiling oil? Tar and feather? A quick call to the lily and a seven-year stretch? Or a touch of your actual rough justice? You just say the word.'

Ashe cringed, and from time to time glanced nervously at Snowey while the General considered his fate.

The moments ticked by.

'It's no good,' Wilson said finally. 'I'm far too angry with you to trust myself to punish you. Go away.'

Snowey could hardly believe what he had heard. His mouth dropped open in astonishment.

And neither could Ashe. He remained there on the stool, stunned.

'Just go away!' Wilson continued.

Ashe didn't wait to be told twice. He got up and ran out of the door before the General had time to change his mind.

Snowey scratched his head in disbelief.

Lucy Cameron sat waiting by her unconscious father's bedside. He had only moved once in a few hours. He hadn't even groaned. Her face was lined with worry. She was glad when Dick Barton and Jock came into the room. She appreciated the company.

'How is he?' the special agent asked with concern.

'They seem to think he'll be all right.'

'That's grand,' Jock commented from the other side of the bed.

'I'd feel a lot grander about it if they had any idea what drug he'd been given.' When she had finished speaking, Lucy bit her lip nervously.

'Still trying to find out?' Barton asked.

Lucy nodded, then she told him the progress that had been made in the past few hours. 'They've sent for a specialist. Meanwhile they're running tests.'

Barton looked closer at the unconscious form on the bed. 'So we've no idea when he might come round?'

'Every blessed doctor says something different,' the girl replied. 'What it amounts to is that they're all stumped.'

Jock Anderson leant across the bed. He knew that Lucy would understand the reason for all these questions. 'We've got to find out whether he gave them the third part of the formula,' he explained.

'Or just fudged it up so as to make them think they had all they needed,' Barton elaborated.

'In which case where is it?' Jock finished.

Lucy followed their line of thinking. 'Any suggestions?' she said.

Barton himself now made a decision. He had been thinking fast. It was unlikely that Muller would let George Cameron get away with anything. 'If he did manage to fool them, they'll be back,' he said. He turned to walk down the ward. 'Stay with him Jock.'

When Dick Barton arrived back at the laboratory, he saw that Snowey was looking pretty bleak. He was sitting on one of the benches kicking his heels against the lockers underneath.

'Snafu rides again,' Snowey remarked.

'What?'

'Situation normal all fouled up,' the ex-sergeant explained.

'Oh. Yes,' Barton agreed. 'If there's one thing I hate it's having to wait for the other side to make the move, but I don't see that we've any option.' He walked over and stood by Snowey's side. 'What did the old boy do to Ashe, by the way?'

Snowey thought about the ex-personal assistant running out of the room like a scared rabbit. 'Blew him a kiss,' he said disgustedly.

'After all that?'

'Near enough,' came the reply. He didn't really want to talk about it. What he wanted now was action. Not sitting about literally kicking his heels while Muller got away with his schemes.

General Wilson then came into the room. 'I say, White, you don't know where we can get hold of . . . ' he stopped talking when he saw Barton, who was now standing by the window. 'Oh, there you are. Thank heaven for that.'

'Trouble?' the special agent said curtly.

Wilson started his usual longest-distance-between-two-points narrative method. 'I haven't been in such hot water since my Passing Out Parade,' he said. 'We buttered the steps, do you see, and the Adjutant rode up them on his horse.' He laughed at the memory and then corrected himself. 'One shouldn't laugh. It was the merest chance the animal didn't damage himself seriously. The Adjutant, too, come to that. Where was I? Oh, yes. The stinking Switzer's named his price.'

'How much?' Barton asked.

'A million pounds.'

'Stone me!' Snowey came down off the bench. He shook his head.

'Pounds. Yes,' Wilson continued. 'In gold at that. My name's mud with the powers that be. My firm, you see. My responsibility. Blasted Muller's wiped the floor with us.'

Snowey had now had time to recover. And, at least the enemy had shown his hand. He was beginning to feel better. 'Then George must have cracked and given him the third part of the formula,' he said thoughtfully.

Barton corrected his assistant. 'Don't get ahead of yourself,' he warned. 'All we know is that Muller thinks it works.'

'He thinks that all right,' Wilson confirmed. 'In fact he's giving a demonstration to convince the government that they'd better pay up.'

Dick Barton was also relieved that things were picking up again. 'Let's get over there,' he said.

'Pick up his trail again,' Snowey suggested.

'Before he can collect, with a bit of luck,' came the reply.

They smiled at each other.

Some time later, Barton, Snowey and General Wilson found themselves plodding over a ploughed field at a location given them by a worried Whitehall official over the phone. They walked towards another group of three men, who were standing looking up into the sky with their hands shading their eyes. As well as the Whitehall man, senior RAF and Army officers were present.

'Here he comes,' said the official, as the whirr of an engine sounded in the distance.

Far away, a dot appeared in the sky. Then, as it loomed nearer, its shape became more distinct.

'We're going to have our work cut out to stay on the trail of that,' Snowey said to the special agent, who was standing by his side.

'Muller wouldn't risk flying it himself,' Barton said. 'If he hired it, it'll be a registered commercial aircraft that we can trace.'

While the others had been talking, Wilson had been keeping an eye on the plane. 'Lysander,' he now announced. 'Used to use them as artillery spotters. Amazing machines. Land and take-off on a pocket handkerchief, near enough.'

The plane now banked, turned, and came in very low over the next field, in which was planted a crop of peas. A fine spray settled over the crop. Then the plane climbed again and soared away into the distance.

'ATL QOBV,' Snowey said. He'd seen the registration number on the fuselage.

'Check,' agreed Dick Barton. 'Get after it.' And then, as Snowey began to retrace his steps across the field, 'And Snowey, stay in touch.'

Snowey waved in reply. He had no intention of making any more bloomers. He was going to find out what he could.

'The spray appears to have no effect,' the Whitehall official said after a while.

General Wilson shook his fist at the retreating plane,

which was now only a speck in the sky. 'Ha, ha ha. Put that in your silly Swiss pipe and smoke it. That'll teach you to suck up to the Pope and yodel and keep goats.'

But, even before the General had finished, Muller's distorted voice boomed over the field. 'Before you celebrate, gentlemen, I should warn you that the substance takes a little while to achieve its effect. When you're satisfied that it does, you will arrange for the *William Tell Overture* to be played immediately after the nine o'clock news.'

Before the voice had started, Dick Barton had noticed a shed in the corner of the field. He was now certain that Muller's amplified tones came from that location. He raced towards it. The General followed as close behind as he could manage.

As Barton came into the shed, the tones became louder, yet Muller himself was not there. Rapidly, the special agent and Wilson began looking amongst a range of agricultural implements and sacks.

'That will be the signal that you are ready to do business on the lines I've indicated,' the voice continued. 'You will then be given your instructions for the payment of the purchase price.'

Barton had narrowed down the location yet again. He expected to find Muller behind a covering of sacks in the far corner, but as he threw them aside he found nothing but an old HMV gramophone with a disc spinning merrily. Fooled by his master's voice, the special agent thought. Only this master was a highly specialised Swiss villain who would stop at nothing.

'Thank you for your attention,' the recording concluded.

General Wilson now joined Barton. He looked at the machine for a moment. 'He who laughs what?' he said.

'He who laughs last, laughs longest.'

'Damn silly remark,' grunted the General.

But not, perhaps, an irrelevant one, the special agent thought to himself.

Snowey White had now traced the possible source of the rented aircraft used by Muller to a small country aerodrome some miles away. It was more club than airfield, he thought, as he nosed around keeping as low a profile as possible.

102

There was a single runway in not too bad a condition, a control tower, two corrugated iron hangars and, further away, a few light aircraft standing in the open. Nearer, some converted Nissen huts served as office accommodation. He'd seen hundreds of places like it before, set up during the war as emergency operations centres, and now crumbling away, or like this one, probably taken over by some enterprising RAF type who didn't want to give up flying.

After closely checking the registration numbers of the aircraft, and finding the Lysander that had done the crop spraying for Muller, Snowey stopped a passing grease monkey.

'Where do I find the mob that flies this heap?' he asked a tall man in oil-stained overalls.

The mechanic didn't say anything. He just jerked a thumb in the direction of the offices. Snowey nodded and began to walk towards them. He was thinking about how he was going to handle the situation. He didn't want to do anything too obvious.

In the hospital room, five figures were grouped around the still unconscious figure in the bed. Dick Barton and Wilson had rejoined Jock and Lucy after it became apparent that there was nothing further that could be done about the demonstration. They had found a consultant peering into George Cameron's eyeballs when they arrived. The man wore a white coat and a lugubrious expression.

'You've got to get him round,' Barton insisted as the consultant finished his examination.

'We are doing all we can,' came the reply.

'He is going to be all right?' Lucy asked anxiously.

The Consultant drew a deep breath. 'I see no reason why not.' There was a pause. 'In the fullness of time.'

'For pity's sake, man, don't you realise,' Wilson said, 'the country's being held to ransom.'

The consultant seemed faintly bored. He spoke slowly, as if he was unable to comprehend the gravity of the situation. 'That's no reason for us to lose our heads, now is it?'

Barton indicated the unconscious scientist. There was no change in George Cameron's condition, but his breathing was at least slow and regular. 'If he was conscious, this man,

103

could help,' said the special agent.

'Thank you,' the specialist replied with over-elaborate courtesy. 'Despite your general incoherence I had managed to get my mind around that.'

Jock Anderson was now angry. Anyone who called Dick Barton incoherent was either a fool or a villain. The consultant was the former, he decided. 'Then why don't you do something about it?' he said sharply.

The consultant retreated behind his official attitude yet again. He grasped the lapels of his white coat. 'More haste, less speed is the first rule of medical science. *Festina lente*, as the Romans had it.'

General Wilson could no longer contain himself. He was nearly apoplectic. 'Blasted Italians,' he roared. 'They're nearly as bad as the Swiss.'

A large car blasted behind Snowey White as he neared the Nissen huts. He had to get off the road and was far from happy about it. He cursed like an ex-trooper, which he was.

When the car stopped in front of the buildings, and a man with a trilby and leather trenchcoat got out, Snowey reacted sharply. He'd know that Kraut anywhere, he mumbled under his breath. It was Klaus.

Snowey waited until Klaus was inside, and then carefully approached the window. He looked in; the place wasn't much, there was a battered table, ex-army filing cabinets, and a peeling pin-up of Vera Lynn on the wall. The forces' sweetheart was looking somewhat neglected.

Klaus was talking to an ex-RAF type who wore a moustache and bandanna.

'Piece of cake, old boy,' the RAF type replied to some mumbled question Klaus asked him. 'Flew there. Squirted the old jungle juice around as per instructions. Beetled back. Money for old rope. Going to tell us what it's all about?'

Klaus's eyes narrowed. 'How many times do I have to tell you?' he began in a heavy accent.

'Keep your hair on,' the RAF type interrupted. 'I hate to rub it in, but you lost the war, you know. So screaming and chewing the carpet old sport . . . '

Snowey turned away from the window. It was obvious that he wasn't going to learn anything much from listening in. He went around the corner of the building again, and stood looking thoughtfully about Klaus's car.

He didn't recognise the make, or the model, or anything about it. 'Oh Jock,' he said softly to himself, 'I wish I'd listened to your rabbiting on now, mate.'

Guns he was all right with, or a Commando issue knife, even landing craft he knew something about. But cars . . . Snowey scratched his head and then made a decision. He approached the vehicle.

The group of four sat expectantly around the bed of the scientist who could tell them how to save the country. They looked up hopefully when the consultant returned carrying a large hypodermic needle.

'Got it licked at last, have we?' General Wilson asked.

The consultant smiled slowly. 'I rather thinks so.'

Lucy looked at her father. 'Oh thank heavens,' she exclaimed.

Even Jock Anderson appeared to have come round. 'Good man,' he said.

The consultant held up the hypodermic so that they all could see.

'All the indications,' he said, 'are that this should do the trick.' Then he rolled back the coverlet and, taking George Cameron's bare arm, expertly gave him an injection.

They all waited with bated breath. Lucy Cameron looked up at Dick Barton's face after a while, but there was no indication of anything at all. She glanced back at her father, he had not even stirred when given the injection, and now, there was still no sign of an improvement.

'Ah, I am rather working in the dark, you know,' the consultant explained.

All Dick Barton replied was, 'Join the club.'

And so they resumed their vigil.

The pilot stood at the doorway to the aerodrome offices. He smiled to himself as he showed the surly German character out. His manner was friendly, but his thoughts were not. 'Righto, old bean,' he said as he waved cheerily. 'You know what they say. Money talks. Or rather doesn't in this case.

Be like Dad, eh, keep Mum.' There was no reply to his remarks. 'Never mind,' he concluded.

Klaus stopped in his tracks and turned. 'You give me away and, I promise . . . '

'Do drone off,' the pilot replied in a less friendly fashion. 'I can't give you away. I haven't a clue who you are. And I've got better things to do than find out.'

Klaus didn't like what he had heard. He started to swear in German.

The pilot didn't quite understand what was happening. 'Honestly, old boy,' he said. 'You're going to blow a gasket if you keep on like this. I've seen it happen.'

And then, suddenly, the RAF type understood. The German pointed towards his car. All the tyres were completely flat.

The pilot walked over to the car and inspected the tyres. He laughed in spite of himself. 'Some bally spiv's pinched all your valves.' He then tried to restrain his laughter. 'What a rotten trick.'

'How am I going to get back?' Klaus asked.

The pilot shrugged. It wasn't really his business. 'Search me,' he said. 'You'll never find four valves. They're rarer than diamonds. I know; took me months to get hold of one for my spare.'

Klaus looked at the pilot. He took out a wad of money. 'I buy your car.'

'Sorry old son,' the pilot explained, but he was laughing inside again. 'Need to toddle off home myself. Little woman and all that. Show up late without the car and I'm liable to get bashed over the head with a skillet. I'll try and get hold of a taxi for you, if you like.'

Klaus thought for a moment. The Herr Professor would not like it if his new headquarters were discovered. And those stupid Dick Barton people were on their trail again. 'I don't want people should know where I go,' he said after a while.

'In that case, my old duck, I can only suggest you walk.'

There was rage in Klaus's eyes as he stamped away.

'And serves you right for being such a surly so-and-so,' the pilot said before he turned and walked back to the offices.

A special phone had been brought in and set up near George Cameron's bedside while the others waited to see if the scientist would recover. General Wilson was talking into it now. There was someone from Whitehall at the other end, with news about Muller's demonstration.

'Say again,' Wilson said excitedly. 'You don't say! Well, I know you do,' he blustered. 'Figure of speech. You're sure? Well, that's the best news I've had all week.' He hung up and turned towards the others, and for once, he came directly to the point: 'Muller's demonstration didn't work.'

'Oh thank God!' Lucy said immediately. She looked as if she might cry.

'Bye!' said Jock Anderson.

'Total flop,' Wilson continued.

Barton voiced the opinion of all of them when he commented: 'What a relief.'

And then, quite suddenly, another voice joined the conversation. 'It couldn't have worked,' it said. The voice belonged to George Cameron. He was now fully conscious.

Lucy was overjoyed. That made two pleasant surprises in less than as many minutes. 'Dad! You're all right!'

The scientist looked around, he hadn't expected so many people at his bedside. Then, he smiled ruefully. 'A bit of a head, but otherwise fine.'

This was the third time that Jock had seen George Cameron narrowly escape from death. The other two had been during the war. And this, the most recent, was also the most vital. 'Well, you have led us a dance,' Jock said. He didn't voice his emotions.

Cameron was slightly more direct. He looked towards his old friend. 'You were the only one I could count on, Jock.' Then, he turned towards the most impressive looking man in the room. 'You'll be Mr Barton,' he said quietly.

'That's right,' came the reply. 'Oh, and this is General Wilson.'

It was now the turn of the older man to receive the scientist's attention. 'None of this need have happened if you'd heeded my letter, sir,' he said.

Lucy held her father's hand while she tried to explain. 'He never got it, Dad,' she said gently. She didn't want him to experience too much of a shock.

'Not your fault,' Wilson felt slightly embarrassed. He was having to admit that Snowey White had been right all along. 'Blame myself for taking on the wrong chap. Ashe, my personal assistant,' he explained. 'That's who the rotten apple in the woodpile was. Or do I mean nigger in the barrel? No matter. We'll make it up to you in any case.'

The consultant, who, up to now, had been content to watch events, now pushed forward. 'If I could look at the patient ... ' he began.

Wilson stopped him. 'Oh, get out man,' he said impatiently. 'You're cluttering up the place.'

The consultant, in spite of his rank and his medical skill, was bustled hastily out of the room.

Lucy now felt able to ask her father the vital question. 'You never gave them the third part of the formula, then?'

'Certainly not.'

'Cameron, I'm proud of you,' the General declared.

Jock Anderson looked up at the ceiling. There was no stopping old Wilson, that was for certain. He was quite relieved when George took up the explanation again.

'There isn't actually a third part as such,' the scientist continued. 'It's all according to the temperature at which you mix the components.' The others seemed to look at him rather blankly, and so he elaborated further: 'It's actually the steam that seems to achieve the fusion. Up until then it's a relatively stable substance.'

The special agent had grasped the salient points immediately; 'A weedkiller, in fact,' he commented.

'That's right,' the scientist agreed. 'I thought if I made Muller a wee sample he'd not be able to do much harm and it might string him along until . . . well – you caught up.'

General Wilson now had nothing but admiration for his employee. In a way, he felt some of the man's obvious competency rubbed off on himself. 'Well done. First rate,' he said.

But Jock was still concerned about the possibility of George's safety in the future. 'What's going to happen now that he knows you've made a fool of him?' he asked.

Lucy also took up the point. 'He's going to come after you, isn't he?' she asked her father.

But, there was someone else in the room who had also been thinking over the probabilities, and he was a man who usually reached conclusions before the others. 'Unless we can get to him first,' Dick Barton said. He continued to think over the matter.

'But we don't know where he is,' Wilson said.

'I hope Snowey's taking care of that,' came the reply. Barton now fully trusted his second-in-command again. It wasn't likely that Snowey would make two bloomers over one affair. And, especially now that Ashe was out of the way, he was expecting results.

Muller's henchman limped along the country road. And there was an expression on his face that said he wasn't very happy about it. He still had several miles to go to a headquarters whose location he wanted to keep secret.

A 1936 Beardmoor taxi chuntered slowly past. Klaus, worn out with walking, finally gave in. He waved it down. The taxi stopped and reversed towards him. The driver, a hard-faced character who was wearing a peaked hat as a nominal sort of disguise, was, in fact, Snowey White. Klaus appeared not to recognise him.

'Where to, sir?' Snowey asked.

'I'll show you,' came the surly reply.

'Threepence a mile, you know, sir,' Snowey warned. 'And double fare beyond the city limits.'

Snowey enjoyed baiting Klaus, and he smiled to himself when the Kraut threw him a wad of notes, saying:

'This should cover it.'

'If the petrol lasts,' Snowey commented as Klaus got into the back of the vehicle.

Then, after he'd started driving again, Snowey glanced back in the rear view mirror to get a better look at his passenger.

Klaus noticed the movement. 'Don't I know you?' he asked suspiciously.

Snowey kept his nerve as the German now began to study him closely. 'I don't think so, sir,' he said casually. 'Mine's a very ordinary sort of a boat race. Face.'

Klaus nodded, but did not seem entirely convinced.

In the front of the Beardmoor taxi, Snowey White drove

on. He wasn't sure that the ruse was going to work. But it was the only chance of tracking down Muller that they were now likely to get. And he wasn't going to let the guv'nor down this time.

Has Klaus recognised Snowey?
Will Muller come after George Cameron before his new hideout can be traced?
Read the next chapter of:
Dick Barton – Special Agent.

Chapter Eight

Swiss villain Gustave Muller has demanded a million pounds in exchange for the formula invented by George Cameron, but his public demonstration failed to work. The scientist has now recovered, and Snowey White is attempting to discover the new secret headquarters of the operation.
Now read on.

The Beardmore taxi driven by Snowey White came to a stop in a clearing. The road stretched on, bending into the trees again, but there were no houses in sight. As Klaus got out of the back, Snowey tried to fix the place in his memory by noticing the main landscape features. It was hopeless; they'd passed dozens of places just like this in the last few miles.

He leaned out of the window and Klaus walked past. 'Nice place you've got here,' he quipped. But there was no reply from the stony-faced German. Snowey tried again; 'Want I should wait for you, guv, or what?'

'No. Go.' Klaus replied surlily.

'You're miles from anywhere here, you know that?'

Klaus then handed Snowey even more money. 'Just go.'

Snowey settled back into the driving seat again. 'You're the customer,' he remarked. He looked for a place up ahead to turn the taxi around.

'That way.' Klaus pointed to the way they had come.

'Whatever you say.' There was no point in pushing it, Snowey realised. Particularly when he wasn't sure that Klaus hadn't recognised him. So, he did a neat three-point turn and began to go back along the unmade road.

But, as he went, Snowey checked the German's progress in his rear view mirror. Klaus was playing it canny. He was standing foursquare in the middle of the road, watching the retreating taxi. Snowey shrugged and drove on. A little further away, he checked again. But the blooming Kraut still hadn't moved.

There was nothing for it but to carry on. He went around a bend, and out of the ex-Nazi's sight.

Klaus watched the taxi disappear. Then, when he was satisfied, he continued to plod along towards headquarters.

But Klaus wasn't the only one who had a few dodges up his sleeve. Once around the bend, Snowey stopped the taxi, and raced back in the direction that he had just come from. He was just in time to see Klaus disappear around another turning. He stopped and thought for a moment. Then he went back to the taxi, and parked it right across the middle of the road. Once more, he hared off after Klaus, only this time he kept under cover whenever possible, and sprinted on the open stretches in short, sharp bursts.

He kept this up for quite a while and eventually came to a fresh section of road. It was in better condition and ran straight ahead for several miles. There were no trees; the country was completely open.

What there was, on one side of the road, was a high stone wall built from square-edged masonry. There was no sign of Klaus on the road. And when he looked more closely, Snowey observed a peculiarly shaped lodge set into the wall at the side of a massive pair of gates. There didn't seem to be anyone around, and there was nowhere else that Klaus could have gone.

He thought for a moment, and, keeping his eyes peeled, moved slowly towards the gates. They were even more impressive from a near view, and made from cast iron sections joined together. Snowey gave them a push, and they moved slowly open without so much as a squeak. Then, after stooping down and picking up handfuls of gravel from the drive that stretched away in front of him, Snowey went in.

Further away, above a clump of trees, he could make out the chimneys of a house. As he walked, he could see more of the place. It was a regular castle, that came complete with turrets, arched windows and even a moat and drawbridge. But, Snowey didn't have much time to enjoy the vista, for at that very moment, he heard the main gates suddenly clang shut behind him.

He spun around very fast, but found himself looking into the muzzles of two guns held by Klaus and a guard. Unheard, the pair had moved up right behind him.

There was only one possible way out of the situation. Snowey tried to carry on with the bluff. 'Oh there you are,' he said to Klaus.

'I knew I knew you,' the reply was hardly original, and it came accompanied by a snarl.

'Never in a million years,' Snowey said. He tried to look as innocent as possible.

'Then what are you doing following me?' Klaus asked as he took a step forward.

'I like that. I was just bothered about leaving you all on your tod. I mean, you'd treated me fair.' Snowey hoped that they were listening to what he was saying and not noticing that he was slowly edging towards them. The fact that Klaus himself had moved helped the situation.

'Stop!' Klaus commanded suddenly. He motioned with the gun.

'Cut it out, will you?' Snowey's manner was hurt. But he was thinking fast.

'Hands up! Up, up, up,' Klaus jerked his gun to emphasise what he was saying.

Slowly, and looking straight ahead, Snowey started to bring up his clenched fists. And then, he suddenly flung the gravel he had picked up earlier into the faces of Klaus and the guard. In the same continuous movement, he chopped the gun out of Klaus's hand, and kicked the guard in the wrist so that he also dropped his weapon.

'Now then,' Snowey said, as both adversaries reeled about blinded, 'Do you want Queensberry Rules or – '

He was interrupted when the guard aimed a karate kick at him. Snowey laughed. It wasn't the first time he'd come across the martial arts, and it probably wasn't going to be the last. They never matched up to the good old unarmed combat technique.

The gloves were off; with a deft movement, he threw Klaus over his shoulder and rabbit-punched the guard. A few more feints, and abortive tackles on their part, and it was all over. They lay on the neat gravel path in a semi-

8   113

conscious condition. The ex-sergeant of commandos smiled to himself.

Meantime, some distance away, a uniformed police constable, who had been cycling along the country road minding his own business, was amazed to find his way blocked by a 1936 Beardmoor taxi which was parked right across the road.

The policeman dismounted from his bicycle, took out his notebook, scratched his head, and then began to take down the registration particulars.

Snowey finished tying up Klaus and the guard, and then securely fastened a gag across their mouths. They glared at him as he emptied their pockets, and then took their guns and ammunition and threw them into the surrounding bushes.

'Don't do anything I wouldn't do if I got the chance,' he said, as he left them, well under cover, and proceeded towards the castle again.

The guard by the castle drawbridge was suddenly alert. He could have sworn that he heard something fall into the water. He listened again, and the sound was repeated. He walked off to investigate.

And while he did so, Snowey, holding his shoes in his hand, promptly bobbed up from the other side of the drawbridge, and raced soundlessly across it and into the castle.

Dick Barton was standing in front of the window at Merton's laboratory wondering how Snowey was getting on, when General Wilson came suddenly into the room.

'Zeta Taxis, for you,' he said.

He was promptly followed into the room by a man who was dressed like a spiv. A bit of a wide-boy, Dick Barton thought. Since the war they seemed to be everywhere.

'The last word in car-hire,' the wide-boy said, interrupting the special agent's thoughts. 'Neat isn't it? My partner dreamed it up.'

Barton looked puzzled for a moment. 'I didn't order a taxi.'

'No,' came the swift reply. It was followed by a wink. 'But your pal did. What a card, eh?'

'Snowey White?'

'Snowey by name, and snow you by nature,' the wide-boy looked pleased with himself. 'Now that's original. I must remember to tell my partner.'

Barton came quickly to the point. 'What did Snowey want?'

More winks followed. 'What didn't he? To tell the truth I thought he was having me on at first.' There was a pause. 'You are Mr Barton?'

'Yes,' said the special agent.

'That's all right then.' A more serious expression crossed the face of the co-owner of Zeta Taxis. 'Very particular our Snowey was that I should tell you and no one else.'

Dick Barton was now becoming impatient. 'Tell me what?'

'I'm trying to, aren't I?' came the reply. The wide-boy gathered himself together again. 'He hired this taxi, see? Only he wanted to drive it himself. Well,' he paused for emphasis. 'It's a bit dodgy with the old insurance, but a bird in the bush – know what I mean?'

Barton turned to the General. 'Do you know what he's talking about?'

'Totally confused,' the other replied. 'Fellow reminds me of myself.'

The wide-boy looked around in an exasperated fashion. 'Listen then, can't you? It's no wonder my partner says conversation is a lost art.'

'It is very important to know where Snowey is,' Barton said slowly and clearly.

The wide-boy nodded sagely, as if there was nothing in the shady line of business that he didn't know about. 'That's why he wanted me to report the cab stolen, wasn't it? So's, if and when the lily found it, I could tell you whereabouts.'

The special agent said one word. 'Where?'

'I am totally and hopelessly lost,' General Wilson confessed. It showed on his face.

'About there,' the wide-boy quipped. He looked at Barton and then Wilson to see if they'd understood.

But the special agent's mind was concentrated on the

115

more serious problem. 'Don't you see?' he said to the General. 'It was the only way he could be sure we'd know where he'd got to.' Wilson still looked blank. 'Muller's new hideout,' Barton elaborated.

Slowly, the General understood. He quickly revised his whole opinion of Snowey White. 'Brilliant,' he offered.

The wide-boy took it as a compliment to himself. 'Well,' he said modestly, 'if you ever need a taxi locally . . .'

'You'll be the last person we think of,' said Dick Barton.

The wide-boy's attitude now began to change. 'Eh?' he replied. 'Oh, I see. I'll have a word with my partner about that.' The last words were uttered as a kind of threat.

Dick Barton didn't want to hang about any longer. 'Let's get over there,' he said to Wilson.

'No, Barton,' the older man replied. 'It's time the police were brought into this.'

There was nothing the special agent could do but consent.

Snowey White was now well inside Muller's grandiose headquarters. He was threading his way past racks of medieval weaponry and suits of armour towards an ornate carved minstrel gallery that overlooked the Great Hall of the castle. Down below, Gustave Muller himself was berating his own scientist.

'I don't take kindly to having plans foiled by ineptitude,' the Swiss declared. 'Still less to being made a laughing stock like this.'

The scientist defended himself as Snowey watched. 'I carried out every step of both parts of the formula,' he protested.

There was a nasty expression on Muller's face. 'Cameron made it work,' he said.

'Then I can only suggest that he used some additional technique which he didn't divulge.'

Muller now showed the full extent of his hatred of incompetence. 'He had no more facilities than you,' he said acidly. 'It would have to be something very simple.'

'It may well be.'

'Then find out!'

All the same, these foreigners, Snowey thought, from his perch up in the gallery, all murder to work for, and liable to lose their temper at setbacks. Talk about lack of patience.

The scientist was now reassuring Muller that things could be put right. 'I shall find out, given time,' he said.

But time was exactly what the Swiss villain no longer possessed. 'Don't you understand?' he thundered. 'After that fiasco the whole country will be looking for us.'

'I'll do my best,' came the reply. 'But, you must understand that, from a scientific point of view, the permutations are virtually endless.'

Muller now frowned and thought for a moment. 'Would we do better to go back to Cameron?'

'That's the only sure short cut,' his colleague confirmed.

Muller stroked his beard while he thought again. It was far from being a situation that was most advantageous. 'But the risk,' he mused. 'They must be guarding that man like the Crown Jewels. Although, of course, you never know with English.' Then he reached his decision. 'All things considered I'm inclined – ' A thought struck him suddenly. His second-in-command was missing. 'Where the devil's Klaus?' he shouted.

His voice echoed in the Great Hall.

Snowey White could have answered that question, and at that very moment someone else was also in possession of that particular piece of information. A new guard had come on duty, and failing to find the one who had preceded him, had begun to search the undergrowth surrounding the castle. It did not take him long to find Klaus and his companion. He released them, and began to run towards the castle to sound the alarm.

Snowey White was wandering in a vast corridor off the minstrel gallery when he heard the alarm bells go. As the sound of commotion came up from below, he began to try the nearest doors. But, he was out of luck, the ones nearest to him were already locked, and further down the corridor he heard others being slammed and keys turning in the locks. He found himself without any cover at all. He wondered what he was going to do.

Muller was still downstairs in the Great Hall when he also heard the alarm. He wondered who the intruders were.

117

'Hm,' he said quietly to himself, 'it seems we have unwanted guests.'

Soon afterwards, Klaus came running into the castle, his heavy footsteps echoing across the floor. He came up to Muller. 'One of Barton's people – ' he began breathlessly.

'How did he get in?' his superior asked immediately.

'He – I – ' a combination of breathlessness and speechlessness temporarily overcame the ex-SS officer.

'Make your excuses later,' Muller said as he dismissed him with a wave. The Swiss psychologist now turned to the guards who were coming from all directions into the hall. 'Search the place,' he ordered.

Eagerly, the minions ran to do his bidding. Urged on by Klaus, they penetrated to the very heart of the castle. Searched the dungeons, the old bakery, even the kitchens. They poked about the corridors, appeared on the roof. Examined all the nooks and crannies and even the secret passages. All with the same result – nothing.

Muller sat alone at the edge of the Great Hall. To an observer who did not know what he was thinking, it would have appeared that he was meditating. Klaus, when he returned to report, was quite taken aback by the quiet self-possession of his superior.

'He can't simply have vanished into thin air,' the ex-Nazi complained.

'We're in a castle, Klaus,' Muller reminded him.

The second in command looked puzzled. 'Herr Professor.'

Muller smiled as if he was talking to a child or an imbecile. 'Where would you hide if you had to?'

Klaus looked around blankly. All he could see in the immediate vicinity were rows of suits of armour, some of which came complete with weapons.

'It's staring you in the face,' Muller continued.

Again Klaus looked around with a puzzled expression. Then, he thought he saw a pair of eyes looking at him from behind a visor. He did a double-take. He had been correct.

'Gott in himmel!' he exclaimed.

Muller smiled sarcastically. 'Congratulations.'

They both turned in time to see a suit of armour containing Snowey White clattering up the stairs.

'Stop him!' Klaus shouted to the guards.

The startled henchmen reacted quickly, and grouped at the bottom of the stairs. Snowey, though encumbered by the heavy iron he was wearing, also carried a mace and chain. Using them to good effect, he managed to clear a way towards the entrance, and made a very noisy exit.

'After him,' Klaus screamed.

The guards rallied, and set off in pursuit. Klaus himself was about to follow them when the castle telephone rang. Klaus picked up the receiver. 'Yes?' His face darkened. He turned to Muller with the news. 'Police at the lodge gate.'

The psychologist still seemed unperturbed. 'It's time we renewed our acquaintance with Cameron in any case,' he said.

The suit of armour was heavy, and, as he lumbered up the drive towards the gates, Snowey thought that he'd change it for a full set of battledress, any day. A beret was a lot more comfortable than a blooming visor.

He glanced back to see the guards coming after him again. There was a nasty clang as a stray shot bounced off his flanks. Another hit him in the small of the back. He didn't feel a thing – there were some advantages.

Suddenly, he heard a shout. When he looked back again, he saw the guards retreating towards the castle. They'd been called off. Still, he continued on his escape route, only to be intercepted near the gates by a Police Inspector, and four members of the Flying Squad.

'Where do you think you're going?' the first of them asked.

'Trust you to be late,' Snowey panted as he stopped. 'I suppose we're lucky you got to the right place.'

The Police Inspector looked dubiously at the man in front of him. It wasn't every day you came across someone in a suit of armour. 'You're under arrest,' he said.

Snowey nodded. 'That's par for the course,' he replied.

'Where are the rest of them?' the Inspector then demanded.

Snowey turned and pointed a steel finger down the drive towards the castle. 'Half way across the country by now, I should think.'

'Look sharp, lads,' the Inspector then ordered his associates. The vast iron gates were opened wider, and police cars, sirens wailing, zoomed in and up the drive.

On the roof of the hospital where George Cameron had lain unconscious, Jock Anderson looked down on a figure in the street below. He was doing his observing with the help of a pair of binoculars. He started for a moment, and then recovered.

'Here he comes,' he called.

Snowey White, now without his armour, crawled along the roof to join the mechanic. He took the binoculars, and focused them on the street below in the direction indicated by Jock.

He saw Klaus's car pull up; the German got out, and walked over to a man who had been keeping watch on the hospital. He had been too casual for a lounger, and Snowey and Jock had spotted him some time before. Klaus then appeared to ask the man for a light, which he received. Then, the ex-Nazi thanked the watcher, went back to his car and drove off.

Snowey handed the glasses back to Jock.

'I thought we had a bite there,' the Scotsman said.

Snowey shook his head. 'Just a look-see.'

In a room in the hospital, Dick Barton and General Wilson were discussing the implications of recent developments with George Cameron and his daughter. The name Muller naturally came high on the list.

'The trouble is he knows we're still about the place,' Barton declared. He turned to the General. 'Perhaps if we were to take our leave ...'

'Oh, thank you!' Lucy interrupted quickly. The thought of being left to the Swiss psychologist's tender mercies again did not appeal to her.

'I mean, of course, appear to –' Barton explained. 'They might just –'

This time it was Wilson's turn to interrupt. 'No, Barton,'

he said decisively. 'I can't allow it.' And there, the General's precision of speech left him. 'I mean to say, we all know life isn't beer and drakes. But you can't play ducks and skittles with people's lives. It's not on.'

The special agent looked closely at the scientist. 'It's up to you, George,' he said slowly.

'That's not fair,' Lucy interrupted again. She felt that her father had done enough.

'How do you feel about playing the tethered goat?' Barton continued.

There was no immediate reply from the scientist. He took time to reach his decision.

'Don't answer that,' Wilson declared. Then he got his constitutions wrong. 'Plead the Fifth Commandment.'

'I can't say I like it,' the scientist said thoughtfully, 'but if they're going to be coming after me in any case . . . ' he paused and glanced towards his daughter, ' . . . it might be as well to be prepared for it.'

'We'll be right behind them,' Barton said reassuringly.

Lucy still wasn't keen. 'Not too far behind this time, I hope,' she added.

General Wilson now adopted a paternal tone. 'You're not getting mixed up in this, young lady, and that's final.'

Lucy shook her head firmly. 'Don't be daft.'

Now George Cameron joined in. He was quite prepared to offer himself as bait, but his daughter was a different matter. 'Now, Lucy . . . '

'And don't you start, George Cameron,' came the swift reply. 'If you'd taken me into your confidence in the first place, we'd have been spared all this.'

Snowey, who had been standing listening to the conversation, now shook his head in bewilderment. 'Women!' he said.

In a more reasonable tone, Dick Barton now spoke to the girl. 'There's no reason for us to involve you in a scrap,' he told her. He meant it; there might be trouble with Muller.

But there was no persuading her. 'Surely, you of all people don't expect me to be logical,' she replied.

Even the General then had to admit that Lucy had won. 'Do you know, Barton,' he remarked. 'I think there's quite possibly no answer to that. Hoist with your own whatsit.'

For once, Barton was beaten by gallantry. He nodded at Lucy. She gave him a winning smile.

Once more, the Riley Monaco came to a halt at the gates of Merton's Fertilizers. The special agent got out of the front, followed by Jock Anderson. Then, Lucy, her father, the General and Snowey piled out of the back.

Viewed from some distance away, it would have appeared to be a touching scene. Fond farewells were exchanged; Barton and Snowey shook hands with Wilson and the Camerons.

Dick Barton had seen the man across the road; he spoke softly to Snowey. 'Got an audience, have we?'

'Old faithful,' came the reply. Snowey had recognised the man. It was the same one who had been keeping an eye on the hospital.

General Wilson had also grasped the situation. As he pumped Barton's hands, he spoke loudly. 'Can't tell you how grateful I am.'

'Only wish I could have done more.'

It was not an elaborate charade, and it was done with enough conviction to make it plausible. Lucy took the opportunity to give Barton a hug. And, as the Barton trio got into the Riley once more and drove off, Wilson, Lucy and George stood on the factory steps waving a fake goodbye.

But the Riley Monaco was only driven around the corner. A pair of garage doors were already open and waiting. The car disappeared swiftly, and the doors were shut tight. Then, Snowey White emerged from a side door and began to work his way back towards the factory.

Workers were now coming out of the factory gates. Concealing himself amongst them, Snowey spotted the watcher across the road. And then, another familiar figure appeared. Snowey smiled as he saw Klaus and the watcher exchange discreet hand signals. Afterwards, the German headed for a call box nearby.

Snowey ducked through the side door and into the garage again. Barton and Jock were waiting in the gloom. 'Looks like he fell for it,' Snowey reported.

Barton looked expectantly at the other members of his team. 'Right, chaps, this is it!'

George Cameron was now back in his familiar workplace. Tibbs was dead, and the laboratory was the same place, and yet somehow different. He was having difficulty coping with a series of conflicting emotions. He had set up some chemical apparatus on the bench, but wasn't really concentrating on his work. Lucy was helping him, and the General, as usual, was talking away about nothing in particular.

'Stinks and Bangs we used to call him,' the General said about his old chemistry teacher. 'Not very original. Bit his nails, I remember. To the quick. Not distracting you, am I?'

'Not in the least,' the scientist replied.

'And, if you could, it would be welcome,' Lucy added with a smile.

Wilson beamed at receiving a compliment from a pretty girl. 'That's the nicest thing you've said all evening,' he remarked.

'They also serve who only reminisce,' Lucy continued.

'Ha!' Wilson came back. He thought for a moment. 'Mark you; I'm not convinced you've got that off pat. But let it pass.'

Lucy looked fondly at her father. They were both glad of the light relief.

Later the same evening, another car approached the factory, only this time the intention of the occupants was much more sinister. The car stopped short of the main gates. Four people got out. They were Muller, Klaus, a getaway driver, and another character whose speciality was forcible entry and kidnapping. Muller looked up at the main laboratory building. There was a single light burning. He knew that George Cameron was inside.

Herman approaches the gate, and in a short space of time he had picked the lock. The getaway driver now went back to the car, and reversed it into the factory yard. Then he shut the gates and arranged them so that they looked undisturbed. When he had finished, he went back and sat in the car. The engine was running. He sat and watched as Hermann, Klaus and Muller now went into the laboratory building.

123

A hand then reached into the car and switched off the ignition. The getaway driver looked up with an expression of surprise. It changed to fear as the hand turned into a fist, and the fist landed in his face.

Jock Anderson was pleased with himself. One down, three to go . . .

Gustave Muller, Klaus and Hermann were now in the corridor. They climbed the steps to the first floor laboratory, making as little noise as possible.

Hermann was last. He looked around as someone tapped him on the shoulder. The only thing he saw was a crooked grin. Then he lost consciousness. Snowey White grinned as the German fell to the floor. A chop to the neck had always been his speciality.

Muller went quietly into the laboratory. No one heard him. George Cameron was intent on an experiment at the far side of the room. His daughter was assisting.

'Mr Cameron,' Muller said quietly.

The scientist spun around. To Muller, he looked completely surprised. The Swiss villain was very pleased with himself. 'My dear young lady,' he said, as he re-introduced himself to Lucy. Then he spoke to Cameron again. 'I must insist that you complete your side of the transaction,' he said.

Someone else spoke from the far side of the room. Muller had not seen him at first. 'And I'm delighted to tell you, sir,' said General Wilson, 'that you've been pipped at the post.'

Muller shrugged urbanely. His confidence was undiminished. 'Please General.'

'You're licked, my dear chap,' Wilson continued. 'Like Jack Spratt. Or his wife. Possibly even his platter.' He paused so that his statement should carry more emphasis. 'The point is, you've walked into a trap.'

'Klaus!' Muller called.

From behind came a voice with a possible imitation of Klaus's accent. 'Herr Professor,' it said.

Muller spun around to find himself facing Dick Barton. The special agent held Klaus in an arm-lock.

'Game, I think,' said Barton. This time, the accent was his own.

'Erich!' Muller shouted frantically.

Snowey White then walked calmly into the room.

'Set, I think,' he said.

'Hermann!' screamed Muller.

Jock Anderson appeared in the doorway. 'And match,' he muttered.

Muller thought for a moment, and then he tried to make a break for it. But, moving incredibly quickly, General Wilson intercepted the Swiss villain and threw him to the ground.

'Good Lord,' Wilson said, as he stood over the defeated, would-be perpetrator of evil. 'Amazing thing the subconscious. I could never have done that if I'd stopped to think about it.'

Muller got up from the floor and dusted himself down fastidiously. Then he reached into his inside pocket, and while appearing to acknowledge defeat, handed over only the first part of George Cameron's discovery. 'Your formula,' he said to Dick Barton. His manners were still perfect.

'Thanks,' the special agent replied, 'but we'll have both parts.'

Muller shrugged, he could see that he was beaten. He did as the man whom he had formerly despised commanded.

Dick Barton then handed both parts of the formula to General Wilson. The Chairman of Merton Fertilizers thought deeply for a moment, and then reached into his pocket for a cigarette lighter. He watched as the formula went up in flames.

'What a waste,' Muller said.

'Better poor than sorry. Isn't that what they say?' asked the General.

'No,' Dick Barton said, 'but I like it.'

The special agent and the old soldier exchanged smiles. Jock and Snowey grinned. Lucy and her father hugged each other. And the defeated Swiss villain, Gustave Muller, gestured in disbelief.

And so 'The Mystery of the Missing Formula' had been solved. It was with relief and a sense of inevitable letdown that Dick Barton, Snowey and Jock returned to London.

As they came into the living room of Barton's Somerset Mansions flat, it was late at night. And the telephone was ringing shrilly.

The special agent walked over to the phone and picked up the receiver. Snowey looked expectantly at Jock.

'Barton. Yes. Hello, Aunt Agatha.' There was a pause, and a look of concern spread over Barton's face. 'Disappeared? I'm sorry, Aunt Agatha, I don't . . . Good heavens . . . Yes. Yes – look don't worry about it – we'll be down first thing in the morning. Not much we could do at this time of night.'

When he had replaced the phone on the hook, Barton turned towards the other members of the team. He didn't really have to say it. 'Looks like we're back in business again.'

'What now, sir?' Snowey asked.

'The case of the disappearing house.'

Jock smiled at Snowey, and the ex-sergeant looked back in puzzlement. What were they in for this time then, Snowey wondered?

They were all soon to find out.

It was the next morning by the time they arrived at the site. Barton, Snowey and Jock were standing with Barton's elderly aunt surveying a pile of rubble that had evidently once been a house.

'I let it about three weeks ago to a young chap named Jenkins,' the old lady called Aunt Agatha explained.

'Jenkins?' said Barton. At the beginning of a case he always tried to gather as much information as possible. You never knew what might be relevant later on.

'Harold Jenkins,' she continued. 'He seemed a nice enough boy and he paid a quarter's rent in advance.'

'And where is he now?'

'I don't know.'

Snowey pointed towards the heap of rubble. 'He's not under that lot is he, missus?'

For a moment, Aunt Agatha seemed quite worried at the thought. Then she brightened up. 'Oh no – the fire brigade searched through the rubble. He seems to have just disappeared.'

126

'Like the house,' said the special agent.

They all looked at the mysterious demolition site once again. There was silence for several moments.

'I don't know what to do,' Aunt Agatha told Barton. 'It was my only income, you see. When your Uncle Wigmore died I moved into the little flat in town and decided to let the house.' The old lady's tone became more and more worried as she went on. 'The insurance company won't pay a penny until they can find out what caused it to collapse.'

'I see,' Barton replied. It was one of the most perplexing beginnings to a mystery that he had encountered. 'All right, Auntie. We'll soon get to the bottom of this. Take Mrs Darblay back to the car, Snowey,' he said to his second-in-command.

'Right you are, sir,' came the reply. 'This way, lady,' he said as he offered a crooked elbow. 'You can take my arm if you like.'

Aunt Agatha was very pleased at such obvious gallantry. 'Why thank you, Mr White,' she exlaimed. 'Thank you so much.'

And, while Snowey was busy leading his aunt back to the Riley Monaco, Dick Barton turned to the third member of the trio. 'Well, Jock? You're the scientific genius of the outfit.'

The Scots mechanic looked thoughtful. 'Bit of a stunner, this, Mr Barton.'

The special agent couldn't have agreed more. 'Isn't it?' he said eventually. Then he stooped down at the edge of the pile of rubble and began to sift through some dust with his fingers.

'Got a wee riddle for you, Jock.'

'Och – I'm nae good at riddles,' the mechanic replied.

'Try this one anyway,' Barton continued as he straightened up. 'When you look at a house what do you see?'

'See?' For a brief moment, Jock thought that Dick Barton was having him on. But then he realised that he wasn't, not on a case like this one. 'Well – you see a roof.'

'Yes?'

'You see walls, doors, windows . . . '

'Good,' Barton interrupted. 'Now look around at this

mess.' He gestured towards the rubble again. 'Any of those tiles missing.'

Jock pointed over to the far corner of the pile. 'Well – there's some roof tiles there.'

'Right.'

'And lots of bricks. I suppose that was the walls.'

'Good.'

Jock now indicated something nearer. 'You can even see a bit of the front door there sticking out – look.'

'Excellent. Go on.'

'What else was there?' Then Jock remembered. 'Oh aye – windows.' He looked around, but he couldn't immediately see any. 'Hmm,' he continued, 'there must be . . .'

Dick Barton watched as the mechanic began to sort through the random pieces of rubble. 'You're getting warm, Jock,' he said with a smile.

Jock then straightened up. He rubbed his chin in a thoughtful manner. 'Well, I don't know, sir,' he commented at last. 'I'd have expected to see broken glass lying about.'

'Exactly, Jock. I've looked all over this site – there is not one single sliver of glass that I've been able to find.'

The two men looked at each other. It seemed incredible. And yet they'd both come to the same conclusion. They wondered why the glass was missing, and what their discovery was going to lead them into.

What is the meaning of the missing glass?
Who is the disappearing tenant of the vanishing house?
Now read 'The Case of the Disappearing House', the next novel in the Dick Barton – Special Agent series.